THE FORGOTTEN FORTUNE
THE JACK REILLY ADVENTURES, BOOK 1

MATT JAMES

SEVERED PRESS
HOBART TASMANIA

THE FORGOTTEN FORTUNE

PRAISE FOR MATT JAMES

For Ernest Dempsey

USA Today bestselling author of
the Sean Wyatt archaeological thriller series

Thank you for your support, friendship, and inspiration

THE FORGOTTEN FORTUNE
The Jack Reilly Adventures - Book 1

By Matt James

PROLOGUE

Mosul, Iraq
2016

After two years of ISIS occupation, American military forces launched a joint operation with the help of French, Kurdish, and Iraqi troops to retake the city of Mosul and forcibly expel the threat. It was a well-coordinated and precisely executed offensive, one that turned the tides in the war on terror.

The late-night air was crisp and dry, and the full moon was high in the sky. If he wasn't constantly looking over his shoulder, expecting to be ambushed at any moment, Jack Reilly would've stopped, closed his eyes, and enjoyed the soft breeze being funneled in through the pitch-black alley.

"Go," he said softly, getting his fellow Delta operators moving.

He and three other soldiers bolted across the street, following closely behind Jack. He led them up the short flight of stairs to the two-story home's front door and kicked it in. His eyebrows lifted in surprise when he removed the partition entirely from its hinges.

I guess they don't make 'em like they used to.

"Contact!" he shouted, snapping his M4A1 carbine to the left. He sent a quick three-round burst into the chest of the living room's single occupant. Unfortunately, the armed man wasn't who they were there for, but he was another high-value target worth getting rid of.

Rifles forward, the four specialists entered the domicile and quickly cleared the first floor. Their intelligence stated that this particular residence was being used as a safe house for a key player within the Islamic State of Iraq and Syria hierarchy, Qasem Azrael, as well as the man's six children. He routinely traveled with them, using them as armed guards as well as his living body armor. Nothing was off-limits to Azrael.

"Friggin' savage," Jack muttered, stepping lightly.

All of them had been seen entering the building ten minutes ago, along with the man Jack just killed.

The household was divided into five rooms; one common area, a small kitchen, and four bedrooms, two of which were upstairs. The team's intel also said that there could be a secret basement entrance on-premise. *That* was the operators' goal.

All was quiet.

"Dammit," Jack mumbled. "Search every square inch of this place."

It didn't take long to clear the entire home. It was evident that Azrael, and his family, had exited through other means. Once they confirmed that the house was empty, they began searching for the hidden access point. Jack came clopping down the stairs from the second story just as one of his men discovered something inside the first-floor master bedroom.

"In here!" Miller called out.

Jack hurried inside. The space held very little in the way of furnishings. A simple dresser, a nightstand, and a bed that sat atop a worn area rug was all that was in the bare room.

Miller was kneeling at the foot of the bed, pointing a small handheld flashlight beneath it. The two men swiftly lifted the drooping mattress from its frame and handed it off to the duo waiting outside the doorway. Now, there was nothing on the floor except for the bedframe and the rug. That's not what interested them, though.

There was a slight, square-shaped lump in the middle of it.

Jack stepped into the middle metal frame and stomped on the lump. It sounded hollow, and it gave a little under his weight. They quickly removed the frame and threw back the rug.

"Bingo," Jack said, reaching for the hatch's metal ring pull.

He stopped, thinking better of it. Backing away, he called, "Hey, Dyson, have a look, will ya?"

The young African American entered the room and dropped to his hands and knees. Rolling onto his side, he did what he was trained to do. Keno Dyson was a sure-handed demolitions expert. He was also well-versed in their applications. In this case, he was looking for a tripwire.

It only took him ten seconds.

"Hello there." He looked up at Jack. "Good thinking, sir."

Jack grinned and waited for his man to disarm the device. The effort only took a minute, but in a mission like this, it seemed like it took closer to an hour. Every second was precious in raids like this. Soon, Azrael's people would figure out what was happening and come to check things out. Jack expected that the guard he had taken out was to check in regularly. It was only a matter of time now.

He glanced over his shoulder and found a pair of boots. The rest of the man was out of his line of sight.

Not this time.

Miller reached for the hatch ring this time. He yanked it open with a shrieking protest of warped wood. Jack got moving, clanging down the utilitarian metal ladder, even before the basement entrance had been made entirely accessible. He descended fifteen feet before finding earth again. The floor was stone, and the room, like the ladder, was unmarkable.

Jack flicked on his rifle's barrel-mounted light and shouldered the weapon. "What the...?"

It wasn't a basement at all.

There were concrete-reinforced passages to the north, south, east, and west. Jack was standing inside the access point of an elaborate tunnel system covertly hidden beneath Mosul.

This was how they moved around the city so fast!

"Ho-ly shit, sir," Dyson said, arriving next.

"Holy shit, indeed," Jack replied, sneering in disgust. The smell was unbearable. Regardless of where the odor was coming from, he stepped away with Dyson to give Miller and Lansing room.

"Uh, which way, sir?" Miller asked, seemingly as confused as the rest of them.

Jack trusted what his gut was telling him and headed north. They moved in a single-file line, keeping their guns pointed away from each other's backs. As always, Jack led the way. He was one of Delta's finest and had served with honor for the last decade. Like so many others, he had been recruited out of the Army. From the day he applied, Jack wanted nothing more than to join one of the Special Forces divisions. And after a brief conversation with a member of the Joint Special Operations Command (JSOC), General Solomon Raegor, Jack knew his calling was with the legendary SFOD-D, the 1st Special Forces Operational Detachment-Delta.

He connected with Raegor the moment he met him, learning a great deal from the man. Unfortunately, five years later, the general passed away from pancreatic cancer. It crushed Jack. He had been the second man in Jack's life to succumb to the disease. First, it was his grandfather, who, like Raegor, had been a great and honorable man.

The tunnel wound like a snake for a quarter of a mile before the team saw natural light again. When they stopped, they also saw movement. Jack raised a fist, stopping his men in their tracks. Then, he signaled them to drop to one knee. They stayed in this position for thirty seconds and watched as a slightly built man disappeared up a ladder similar to the one they had descended.

No, not a man, Jack realized. It was a boy.

"Azrael is here."

Jack stood, signaling his men to do the same. They moved toward the exit, keeping their pace steady and controlled. As fiendish as the ISIS leader was, Azrael's death could wait until the opportunity properly presented itself. They were trained never to rush into anything.

He slowed and carefully stepped over a pile of rubble. It contained equal parts of brick and stone. The damage had been caused by the passage's builders. They had forcefully broken through the wall of the local sewer system to connect their tunnel network to it.

Ugh, Jack thought. *So, that's what that was!*

Jack slung his carbine over his shoulder and ascended the ladder without haste. Above his head was an open manhole. It allowed the moonlight in. It was the light Jack had spotted earlier. He had some past experience with maintenance hole covers. They were hard to move for a grown person, let alone a child.

In one motion, Jack drew his sidearm and rocketed his head and right arm out of the opening. Up ahead was an alley similar to the one they had been in minutes earlier, at the beginning of their night raid. In the soft, flickering glow of a bent streetlight, Jack saw the same boy disappear across a road, and then reappear on the other side. He ducked through a second, artificial light source and then vanished into the shadows beyond.

But before he slunk away, the youngster glanced back the other way. Jack ducked back into hiding, leaving just his head above the surface. The child's eyes stopped on Jack, though he wasn't positive if the kid did, indeed, see him, or not.

Slowly, he lifted himself entirely out of the sewer, keeping his pistol pointed forward. Seeing nothing, he holstered his sidearm and opted for his heavy-hitting M4, a weapon with far superior accuracy. He kept the barrel light off and used his keen eyesight to his advantage.

A shadow twitched further ahead. Was the boy baiting him, or was he scared and in need of a rescue?

Shit... Jack didn't like this.

"Move," he whispered without checking the location of his teammates first. He knew they were already in position behind him. He loved these guys. They were always exactly where he needed them to be.

Unlike the child, the four operators avoided the first streetlight, ducking behind a pair of burned and bombed-out vehicles before attempting to cross. Jack held out his left hand and slowly bounced it up and down as if he was leisurely dribbling a basketball. The motion was for his people to move at the same speed. Then, he jabbed a thumb into his chest.

"Me first."

Dyson, Lansing, and Miller weren't happy. They *never* separated from one another. It was too dangerous for multiple reasons, especially when they were deep into enemy territory.

Halfway across the charred street, Jack was forced to step around random car parts. There was a half-melted tire, most of a spiderwebbed windshield, and a car door, among other nondescript items.

Jack paused when the boy stepped into the light. The child shook, and his eyes were on his own feet, not the armed American in front of him. He was terrified. With nowhere to hide, Jack stopped and lowered his rifle.

It was a mistake to do so.

"Hey," Jack said, speaking in Arabic, "are you okay?"

The child didn't reply. The only answer Jack got was a pair of sad, helpless eyes as he looked up at him. Then, the boy did the unthinkable. He raised his right hand and showed Jack something. It wasn't a gun...it was something far more dangerous.

It was a detonator.

Tears streaked down the kid's face. Jack did the humane thing and lowered his carbine, going as far as setting it down on the road. He lifted both hands and spoke softly.

"Take it easy. You don't have to do this."

The boy sniffed. "I do... I will not go back to him." He choked back a sob. "I...can't."

What did he do to you?

The child raised his hand, and Jack did the only thing he could do. He wasn't going to shoot the boy. He couldn't live with himself if he did. So, Jack reached for the mangled car door and lifted it in front of him just as a burst of sunlight exploded to life. The blast threw Jack backward. He landed with the smoldering car door laying on his chest. Jack tried to climb to his feet, but he couldn't, and it wasn't just the half dozen injuries he sustained that prevented him from moving.

It was also his soul.

Jack didn't care that the mission was a bust. Eventually, Qasem Azrael would come to justice. All he cared about was the little boy who had lived a rotten life—one that was so bad that he'd rather kill himself than return to his father.

Jack laid his head back with tears freely rolling down his face.

He was done with the military.

1

Wyoming, USA
Present Day

The five-hundred-pound Grizzly bear reared up on its hind legs, towering over the two men with ease. At its tallest point, the animal easily exceeded nine feet in height. The duo had stumbled upon the mother and her two cubs while looking for a lost hiker. Now, they were the ones that needed rescuing.

Fred Osman, the missing sightseer, was last seen only two days ago in the area. His cellphone's signal had died six hours ago, leading Yellowstone National Park ranger, Jack Reilly, to believe that the man had been seriously injured, or possibly had died. It would be rare to find a person alive given how long he'd been gone, especially with an overprotective Grizzly on the grounds.

Well, I guess we know what killed Mr. Osman, Jack thought, still as a statue.

Neither he nor his partner, Tatanka Durham, looked the beast in the eyes. Instead, they kept their lines of sight low. Both men held semi-automatic AR-15 rifles at the low-ready just in case the animal charged. The firearms were standard weapons for this exact reason. So far, they had avoided conflict, but only because they were trained to deal with such adversities.

Tatanka's name translated to "buffalo" in the Lakota Native American language—his people's language. So, naturally, when Jack found out what it had meant, he started calling Tatanka "Bull" because of the man's first name's affiliation with his last.

Bull Durham was one of Jack's favorite movies. The 1988 comedy revolved around the Durham Bulls minor baseball team. One of Jack's favorite quotes was when Kevin Costner's "Crash" Davis dared Tim Robbins' "Nuke" LaLoosh to hit him in the chest with a ball. Nuke laughed at the ridiculousness of the taunt and warned Crash that, if he did, he could kill him. Straight-faced, Crash replied with, "Yeah? From what I hear, you couldn't hit water if you fell out of a fucking boat."

"Steady," Jack whispered, speaking to himself more than anyone.

Bull said nothing because he typically said very little. Bull's people were one with nature, including being silent when at all possible, and enjoying her sweet song.

The sway of the tall grass.

Rain striking the surface of a pristine lake.

The playful chirping of birds in a secluded forest.

Bull was a skilled tracker. Jack's expertise was in search-and-rescue. Together, the duo was formidable against anything Yellowstone threw at them. They rarely failed.

The Grizzly had other ideas.

Her low, guttural bellows genuinely frightened both men. Even as seasoned as they were, the raw power of a creature like this one was nothing to take lightly. If she wanted to, the female could charge them, reaching speeds above thirty miles per hour. No matter how hard they tried, Jack and Bull wouldn't be outrunning her.

Neither man wanted to shoot her.

So, they stood their ground and patiently waited. Typically, bears backed down if left unprovoked. Mama bears were tricky, however. They tended to go above and beyond when their cubs were around.

The only other option might be to use the extra-large pepper spray "pistol" holstered on his right hip. It reminded him of a pint-sized fire extinguisher. The high-velocity spray cannon, if aimed right, would successfully deter the animal.

The trick to using it was to allow its recipient to get close.

Fat chance, Jack thought.

The Grizzly didn't deserve to die. She was doing what all mothers would do: Protecting her children. Jack and Bull, and possibly their missing hiker, not her, were the trespassers here. But with every passing second that she didn't give up and turn away, Jack was worried that her death was inevitable.

"Get ready," he said, looking up.

As soon as his eyes found the bear's, she roared. Jack had just become her rival. He had done it on purpose, however. Even though the female was smart, she wasn't a person—and she wasn't a person like Jack Reilly.

The pair of cubs responded and slunk away into the brush behind their mother. Slowly, Jack shouldered his rifle, but he kept his finger off the trigger.

Like a torpedo being shot out of a submarine, the bear dropped to all fours and charged, head down. She focused on her closest foe: Jack.

But he had an ace up his sleeve. He knew more about the bear than she did about him. Grizzlies were surprisingly agile creatures despite their imposing size. The species had a bite strong enough to crush a bowling ball too. Jack was more interested in this one's body weight, though. That, combined with its impressive sprint speed, made the bear more of an out-of-control, toothy boulder than a light-footed ninja contortionist.

With only feet to go, Jack shouted, "Now!"

He dove left, and Bull dove to the right. The Grizzly frantically tried to change course but couldn't, stumbling and going down. She barrel-rolled into, and through, a thicket of shrubs, disappearing from view. Instead of getting closer to the bear himself, he let the animal do all the work.

The pair quietly got to their feet and carefully listened. The rangers slung their rifles over their shoulders and drew their pepper spray pistols. They could hear the creature wrestling around in the entanglement, although she hadn't yet emerged to re-engage. *Shit.* Jack would never forgive himself if she were hurt.

Slowly, he crept forward while Bull hung back.

There were only three feet between him and the brush. With a lightning-fast swipe, the Grizzly's enormous paw lashed out through the thicket, knocking the pepper spray from Jack's hand. One of her immense claws cut his wrist to boot. He swung his carbine up and around and ripped it aside as well. Then, the bear emerged.

And she was pissed.

Unarmed, Jack backed away slowly, quickly starting to panic. Looking over his shoulder, he saw that Bull had his rifle jammed firmly into his right shoulder. He stalled the man's attempts at shooting the animal with a raised hand. Jack pleaded for more time to get out of this without either him or the Grizzly, getting hurt. Bull was also the last person that wanted to harm a living thing. He valued the existence of the Earth's inhabitants more than most.

Jack had spent the better part of his adult life bumping off a sect of them. Nevertheless, his conscience was clear. He went to bed knowing that the people he X'd-out maintained despicable existences. He specialized in silencing people who took joy in harming others. Now, he was in the profession of preserving life. Everything in Yellowstone was the responsibility of park rangers like him. The animals, plants, rocks, and people within the United Nations Educational, Scientific, and Cultural Organization (UNESCO) World Heritage Site were under the protection of Jack's employers, the National Parks Service (NPS).

On her back legs once more, the Grizzly pushed through brush, snarling like a demon. The rage on display was remarkable. Jack would've loved nothing better than to watch her from afar, but instead, he was right in the thick of it.

When she dropped to charge Jack again, he closed his eyes and waited for it to be over. Either he'd be killed, or he'd be gravely injured. Regardless, he was about to experience a Grizzly mauling up close.

Amazingly, it didn't come.

Jack was startled when he and the bear were doused in pepper spray. The concoction instantly caused him and the animal to cough and gasp for air. He inadvertently took a deep breath to yelp and took in a small amount of the aerosolled brew. In doing so, he'd experienced first-hand what it was like to be on the other end of his pepper cannon.

The bear whined, whimpered, and fled, crying like a scolded puppy. Her cubs hurried along after her, skirting around Jack and the remaining spice-filled cloud. With his eyes clenched shut, Jack grabbed at his left side. Tilting his head skyward, he drew another piece of equipment, perhaps the most vital one he carried. He unscrewed the cap of his canteen and splashed his face a half-dozen times, clearing away the worst of the remnants.

Opening his eyes, he sighed and turned. Bull wasn't pleased, but he didn't voice his displeasure. His deep scowl said enough. Jack had just forced Bull to harm one of nature's creations.

"My bad," Jack said, scratching his head. "I pictured that going a lot better in my head."

Finally, the corner of Bull's mouth curled into a small smile. He rolled his eyes and holstered his spent pepper spray pistol, picking up Jack's discarded carbine in the process. Through tear-filled eyes, Jack located his own pepper cannon eight feet to his right.

"You underestimate her might," Bull said, his baritone voice rumbling like thunder.

"Who, mama bear?"

He shook his head. "No, the natural world. She is unpredictable and does not bow to man's will so easily."

Jack knew he was right. Even after working as a park ranger for the last four years, he still couldn't get used to the fact that he wasn't in control. This was nature. It wasn't a well-coordinated military strike. Out here, humanity wasn't in charge.

Mother Nature was.

Bull had been a great mentor to Jack thus far. He was an even better friend. He had once given Jack two handmade bracelets after he had learned about the soldier's past. They symbolized Bull's admiration for men like him. Jack appreciated the gesture a lot. Not everyone understood why some people served. Even a handful of them had thought Jack was a moron for willingly putting himself in mortal danger.

Bull had never asked him why he fought against terror. All he had done was thank him for his service. A few months after receiving the gifts, it all made sense. It turned out that Bull's late father had been a veteran.

The beautifully beaded bracelet on his left wrist symbolized "strength," while the one around his right wrist represented "courage." Jack happily put them on, and he'd yet to take them off since. If it were up to him, they'd never leave his body.

After washing his face off again, Jack and Bull got on their way. Mr. Osman was still missing, and they needed to confirm his whereabouts before sunset. If they didn't, the chances of them finding him would be slim-to-none. The park was too vast. Rarely did someone stay in one place for too long. Usually, they'd ramble around until they became exhausted and dehydrated.

That's where Jack was leaning.

The telltale chirp of Jack's satellite phone interrupted their search. He slowed and removed it from the side pocket of his backpack. The number that appeared was that of their main office. Usually, it was the field man who'd be calling the office, not the other way around.

He answered. "This is Jack."

"Hey, Jack, it's Sally." She wasn't as bubbly as usual.

Sally Siling was the main cog in their team's machine, mostly handling the dispatching duties. She also coordinated their efforts with local law enforcement. Sally was the bridge between the NPS and the rest of the world.

"Hey, Sal, what's up?" Jack asked, concerned. "Everything good back at HQ?"

"Everything is fine here." She sighed. "Jack, we just got a call." Her voice was shaky. "Since you were in the field, we couldn't guarantee them how long it would take to reach you, so we took a message and—"

"Sal," Jack interrupted. There was absolutely something wrong. "What's going on?"

"I'm so sorry, Jack. It's your grandmother..."

2

Auschwitz-Birkenau State Museum
Oswiecim, Poland

Agatha Reilly, born Agatha Catherine Strzempka, was a remarkable woman. The Polish schoolteacher, turned historian, adopted Jack when he was six, following her son and daughter-in-law's deaths aboard a single prop airplane. Jack's parents were taking an aerial tour of the Nazca Lines in Peru when they went down due to engine failure.

Along with her husband, Philip Ernest Reilly, a World War II veteran of the British Army, Agatha raised Jack in a household chock-full of archaeological and military history. The Reillys immigrated to the States a few years after getting married. Philip had become a successful stock trader, and Agatha had taken a job with the Smithsonian. The pair eventually retired, comfortably, in their late fifties after Philip hit it big on a couple of investments.

Jack's grandmother—his *babcia*—developed a love of history following her time as a prisoner in the most well-known Nazi concentration camp of all, Auschwitz. Hitler's ruthless Gestapo had kicked in her family's door when she was a teenager, arresting her and her parents for nothing more than being Jewish. It was the last time she ever saw her mom and dad.

Agatha was a determined and inquisitive woman from the very beginning. She questioned everything, a trait that most found unappealing in her day. It wasn't until she met a British soldier, named Philip, following the liberation of Auschwitz that Agatha found love. The pair later found out that they may have met once before, though, unlikely. Philip had been there that day—the day Agatha and thousands of other prisoners had been liberated from their terrible bondage. It was the day Auschwitz was shut down for good by the Allied Forces.

That was a great day.

Jack owed everything he was to his grandparents. They happily took him in and raised him as their son, not just their paternal grandson. Jack's father, Phil Jr., a freelance photographer, had sold his work to major news outlets and magazines, globally. He and Jack's mother, Stephanie, were combining a work trip to Peru with their tenth anniversary when they tragically perished.

Jack blinked his eyes, pulling back the tears that threatened to fall. He remembered the phone call as if it were yesterday.

His grandmother answered the phone like it was any other day. He often stayed with them, something he gladly did whenever his mom and dad traveled. He loved staying in his grandparent's home. It was filled wall-to-wall with historical finds—a miniature museum that any young lover of history would enjoy. Jack grew up wanting to be exactly like Philip and Agatha.

He loved the stories his grandfather told him about the days when he served.

A young, wide-eyed Jack would sit and listen to his grandmother go on and on about the places she traveled to and the things she saw. Agatha never got enough of Jack's questions, even after she retired.

Regrettably, he was only able to study under his grandfather for another decade. Philip passed away when Jack was still in high school. It was his death that spurred Jack to enlist in the United States Army. He wanted to honor the man's legacy, a man that fought valiantly against the worst of the worst, the Nazis.

Philip had heroically stormed Normandy Beach and then went on to help liberate Auschwitz. He was a war hero, but he had never looked for a pat on the back. Jack's service with Delta was very much the same. They didn't look for recognition, or fame and fortune. Soldiers didn't need the public spotlight to be prideful in what they did. Jack and the other operators did the job because a job needed to get done. Period.

The cold breeze snapped Jack out of it. It was nearly winter in Poland. The temperatures were already in the thirties, and a light snow dusting was present from time to time. Their young guide, Kasper, had given Jack and two dozen other patrons a haunting walking tour of the main camp. He'd learned so much about what the prisoners had gone through while confined here.

What Grandma went through, he thought, picturing a teenaged Agatha Strzempka marching in line to the Women's Barracks.

There were also the Prisoner Reception Center, the crematoriums, the communal latrines, and of course, the gas chambers. It was all awful, but it was essential for people to learn about so they could avoid a repeat offense.

Jack broke away from the tour early to meander in peace. He weaved in and out of other tour groups and took in as much as he could. Most of the centralized red brick buildings were once used as barracks for the Polish Army before the complex was overtaken and transitioned into the main camp and administrative headquarters for Hitler's people.

Electrified barbed wire fencing, the same fences used during the war, were still present. Just their presence made Jack uncomfortable—as did the brisk breeze slapping his face. Luckily, the sun was out. He tilted his head up and caught a few of its rays.

"Enjoying yourself?"

Jack opened his eyes and turned around.

A beautiful woman with shoulder-length blonde hair was watching him. Her eyes were a crystal blue, amazing to look at, and based on her accent, she was a Brit, though her accent hinted at some other European influence. Jack grew up with a British grandfather. He was very accustomed to its nuances.

They were alone at the barbed wire fence. Everyone else had moved on to find something more interesting than a rusty, wire fence.

Jack shrugged. "Considering where we are, yeah."

"You don't like this place?" she asked, adjusting the wool beanie on her head.

"No, do you?"

She nodded. "Yes, but only because I'm writing a paper on it."

That made more sense to Jack than just loving the concentration camp because of what it was. She was clearly a student, though, she looked a little old to be in college.

Early thirties, maybe?

"Thesis?" he asked, honestly interested.

"Yes, I've been studying this place from afar for over a year." She looked around. "I'd be lying if I said that I wasn't excited to finally be here. My family was involved in the war, like most. I needed to see this place with my own eyes."

"What school do you go to?"

"The University of Bonn in Germany. After a career change, I decided to move and study what I've always been fond of, the history of the Second World War." She laughed. "Better late than never, I suppose."

Jack knew what she meant.

"I can relate."

"Oh?" she asked.

He nodded. "I'm a park ranger in Yellowstone. Before that, I was in the military."

"Afghanistan?"

He wiggled his hand. "A little. I was mostly in Iraq."

"And Auschwitz interests you because...?"

"Um, well, you see, my grandma was a prisoner here towards the end of the war. She passed away last month, and I thought this would be a great way to remember her."

The blonde smiled. "I gather you were close."

"We were," Jack replied. "My grandparents raised me. Grandma was a pretty well-known historian with the Smithsonian back in the States. Everything I am is because of her and my grandpa."

She stepped up to him and held out her hand. "Emma Schmidt."

He clasped it. She had a firm handshake. "Jack Reilly."

"It was nice to meet you, Jack."

"Likewise."

She turned but swiftly stopped. "Maybe, if we bump into one another again, we can get a cup of coffee?"

He shivered and nodded. "Yeah, I'd like that."

Jack hadn't come to Poland to meet new people, including beautiful blonde Brits. Yet, here he was, in Auschwitz, doing precisely that. He didn't let it consume him, though. The chances of him ever seeing Emma again were slim to none. In a week, he'd be back in Wyoming, searching for another lost tourist.

He and Bull did eventually locate Mr. Osman. He was perfectly fine too. The story goes that Mr. Osman bolted from his house one night, panicked and scared...after his wife learned of his workplace affair with his secretary. He'd been hiding out in the park too terrified to go home to his, understandably, irate spouse. She reported him missing after not coming home for a second night. Jack had almost been torn to shreds by a Grizzly for nothing.

As soon as Jack turned his attention back to the fence, and off of Emma's tight butt, he heard the last thing he ever thought he'd hear. Gunfire. The screams of museum visitors quickly followed, as did the echoing report of additional gunshots.

Multiple shooters, he deduced. *Same caliber rifle too.*

Jack wasn't sure if there was anyone around to fight back. He recalled seeing a small security presence on the grounds, but nothing to write home about. He'd seen three men stationed around the camp so far. None carried anything harder hitting than a nightstick and a stun gun.

Seriously, who'd want to attack a museum?

"Jack?" Emma shouted, confused. She also sounded scared.

He rushed to Emma's side and grabbed her by the back of her arm. Quickly, he half-dragged her out of the open and into a tight alleyway separating a row of brick barracks. More screams arose. In response, Jack moved faster, finding the nearest accessible building he could: Crematorium I.

Previously used by the Polish Army as a munitions bunker, the brick and concrete building was responsible for thousands upon thousands of deaths. It was incredibly eerie that he and Emma were seeking shelter there now.

So far, the Brit was holding it together pretty well. He needed to keep her that way for as long as possible. He wouldn't be able to protect her effectively if she turned into a blubbering mess.

"Okay," he said, entering the first room on the right, "this is what's going to happen... We're going to hole up here for as long as we can. If we have to leave, then we'll do so quickly and quietly. You," he squeezed her arm tighter, making sure he had her full, undivided attention, "will do everything I say, okay?"

Emma silently nodded, eyes wide.

"Wh...what did you say you did in the military?"

He shook his head, peeking through a shoulder-height window. "I didn't say, but if it makes you feel better, know that I handled people like this all the time."

"What people exactly?"

He glanced over his shoulder. "Terrorists."

"How do you know they're terrorists?"

Jack shrugged. "Call it a hunch." He moved deeper into the building. "I usually have a pretty good feeling about things like this."

"Like wh—"

"Look," Jack interrupted. His frustrated outburst made the woman jump. He needed to cut her some slack. Emma wasn't him, and he needed to remember that. "Look..." his voice was calm, "we're in a place with no intrinsic value besides a historical one. Terrorists use unnecessary force to prove a point. They aren't here for any other reason than making a public scene, but they need a bargaining chip for anyone to stop and listen."

Her eyes opened wide. "Us... Hostages."

He pointed a finger at her and winked. "Bingo."

Jack headed through the next doorway on the left. On the other side was a large, empty rectangular space. Twenty feet further ahead was another doorway. He took a second left and stepped into a brick room filled with ovens. This was where the Nazis had burned the bodies.

It gave Jack the chills.

The door to the crematorium creaked open. The person responsible for opening it didn't sound too friendly either, screaming at another man loudly...and he did it in German.

What? Jack thought, trying to work it out. *Why is a group of armed Germans taking over Auschwitz?*

Their hunter could be heard moving deeper into the crematorium. His footsteps were noisy and easy to follow. The acoustics, along with the tight confines of the building, made the former counter-terrorism specialist grin.

"What's so funny?" Emma whispered.

Jack didn't answer.

He put a finger to his lips and flattened himself up against the wall just inside the oven room. The guy with the gun didn't know *Jack* about who else was in the building.

3

The room held four ovens in two sets of two. They were positioned so they looked like a pair of *equals* symbols sitting end to end with a gap in the middle. Emma hid behind one of them while Jack waited for the gunman to show himself. The man's grinding footfalls sounded like shotgun blasts in the bunker-like structure. It was the only sound of any kind.

Jack's practiced patience paid off. The tip of an assault rifle poked its way through the opening to his right. Jack instantly recognized the German-made Heckler & Koch HK416. It was a beast of a weapon.

These guys are pros, Jack thought. No way would an "activist" be armed with a carbine like that.

As soon as the weapon appeared, Jack launched himself forward and lashed out with a front kick, driving the gun barrel away. Jack was now perpendicular to the enemy. He quickly sidestepped deep inside the other man's reach and uncorked a devasting elbow strike into the German's right orbital bone. Jack followed with a left knee rise into the man's groin, dropping him to his knees. It also made him drop the weapon.

Jack snatched it up and backed away, shouldering it like the pro he used to be. Seeing her savior in possession of the intimidating rifle, Emma stepped out and joined Jack across the room.

"Who are you?" Jack asked. "What do you want?"

The lower half of the man's face was covered in a tactical face mask. All Jack could see was the top half of his head and his vengeful eyes.

Jack stepped closer, jaw tight. "Who are you?"

Emma stepped forward and asked the man the question in flawless German.

Jack looked at her, confused.

"Three years of German in secondary school and even more when

I moved to Bonn," she explained.

The disarmed shooter eyed her for a second longer and then spoke. Emma translated for Jack.

"We're here for what's ours," she said.

Jack had no idea what that meant. There was nothing in Auschwitz except for bad memories.

"And that is?" he asked.

The terrorist's cheekbones rose slightly. He was smiling. "The *Fuhrer's* fortune."

Jack's right eyebrow lifted. He glanced at Emma, who shrugged. She had no clue, either.

"What fortune?" he asked.

The German's eyes narrowed. "The forgotten kind."

He explained further, speaking quickly, and Emma did what she could to keep up.

"He says that there is a hidden trove of wealth somewhere between here and the mountains to the northwest. He also says he's supposed to meet his commanding officer here and await further orders."

"Hold up," Jack said, recalling something he read about years ago. "He doesn't mean the gold train, does he?"

Emma asked.

"*Ja,*" the mercenary replied, nodding.

Jack burst out in laughter. "Sorry to burst your bubble, *Hans*, but it doesn't exist. People have been looking for that train for decades and have come up with less than bupkis. I even studied it for a bit because it sounded cool. The research was fun, but that was about it. It's a complete waste of time."

The man had the gall to laugh back.

"What's so funny?" Jack asked.

The shooter quieted and turned his attention to someone else—to Emma. He spoke to Emma in German. It didn't bother Jack that the two conversed. What bothered him about the exchange was that it was cordial—friendly, even. It was like the two of them knew each other.

Damn.

The confiscated carbine suddenly felt like it weighed a hundred pounds. He was screwed. So, Jack relaxed his stance and slowly turned his head. The muzzle of a pistol was only inches from his face.

"Emma?"

The woman grinned. "Sorry, *Herr* Reilly."

Now, her inflection was heavily German.

The male mercenary got to his feet. He was as tall as Jack, maybe six-two, but was thicker than he was, somewhere around 220 pounds. He aggressively tore the weapon from Jack's hands and turned it on him once more.

"But like my brother said, he was looking for his commanding officer."

"Hang on..." Jack said, shocked, "you're leading this boy band?" He slowly raised his hands and took a step back.

She smiled like a Great White. "*Ja.*"

"And why exactly are you doing this?"

"Mine and Gunter's great-grandfather worked closely with the extraordinary Heinrich Himmler, leader of the *Schutzstaffel*. He was Himmler's personal assistant, Elias Schmidt—a man that knew everything the *Reichsfuhrer* knew."

While taking it all in, Jack smartly allowed himself to be tossed against the wall and cuffed with zip ties. He'd willingly play ball until the time was right. As long as he was alive, he stood a fighting chance. So did the people outside.

While Emma trained her gun on him, Gunter thoroughly patted him down, finding nothing except for his rental car keys, wallet, passport, and hotel keycard. He took them all.

Jack sighed. *Dang.*

Then, Emma's brother grabbed Jack by the back of his shirt and forced him to the front of the crematorium. He threw open the door and tossed him outside. Jack tumbled to a stop and was quickly surrounded by a foursome of identically dressed men. Each one of them was outfitted in the same manner as Gunter. They wore all-black fatigues with facial masks that hid their identities. The only one that was dressed down was Emma. She was out there for everyone to see.

"I had you pegged wrong," Jack said, struggling to his knees. "I kinda thought you were cool."

Emma stood before him, pistol holstered, hands on her hips.

"And now?" she asked, unfazed.

Jack looked around, taking in his audience.

"Now, I think you're a bitch."

Gunter drove the stock of his rifle into the side of Jack's head. It sent him sprawling to the ground, groaning in pain. Blinking away the spots in his vision, Jack decided it was in his best interest to stay down. He'd make them carry him if he was to be left alive.

Looking up at the sunny sky, Jack laughed. "Geez, you hit like your sister."

Gunter stepped up to him, blocking out the sun with his thick upper body. He raised his carbine again. Just when he was about to hit Jack again, he was stopped.

"*Halt!*"

Gunter kept his weapon raised, but snapped his head to the left, angry that Emma had stopped him. Jack was grateful, but there was no way in hell that he was going to thank the witch. Emma joined her brother, gazing down at Jack like a pair of circling vultures. She shared a look him with—a look that didn't sit right with Jack.

"We mustn't harm him." She leaned on her knees. "Jack is going to help us find our train."

Jack's dam ruptured, and he burst out in laughter, unable to hold it back. It didn't last, though. Gunter drove the tip of his boot into Jack's ribs. He groaned, cringing in pain. He took a couple of deep breaths and laughed again.

"Damn, *Hans*, are you wearing Steel Toes? That was like getting kicked by an *ass*!'"

"Laugh it up, Jack," Emma said, her tone serious, "but you will help us."

He snorted. "In your dreams, lady."

She brushed away a loose strand of hair from her face and tucked it behind her left ear. "I've been generous, Jack. There have been no lives lost. But, if you don't help us, I'll start killing hostages one by one...starting with the women and children."

"*Oben!*" Emma yelled.

Two of the newcomers slung their identical Heckler & Koch rifles over their shoulders and pulled Jack to his feet. Emma confidently strolled up to him until she was only inches away.

She trained her piercing blue eyes on him. "Welcome, Jack Reilly, to the beginning of the Fourth *Reich*." She lovingly stroked his cheek with her hand. "I'm proud to have you as my project leader." She grinned. "You look like a man that can get the job done, because, remember, if you don't..."

Jack knew when he was beaten. "If I help you, what guarantees do I have that you won't harm anyone?"

"None," Emma replied, "but I hardly think you're in any position to make demands."

Now, it was Jack's turn to smile. "That all depends on how desperate you are for my help."

Gunter slammed the stock of his carbine into Jack's gut, dropping him to his knees. He couldn't breathe as a result. His core had taken a beating in a matter of minutes. Jack desperately gasped for air but was unsuccessful, and just when his breathing was getting under control, Emma gave another order in German, and Jack was clubbed from behind.

His eyes rolled into the back of his head, and he blacked out.

Jack felt like he'd been hit with a sledgehammer. One of Emma's background dancers had pistol-whipped him from behind. Now, he'd like nothing more than to return the favor. But to do that, the world needed to stop spinning.

Groggy, he slowly opened his eyes, wincing against the intensity of the afternoon sun. The crisp breeze hit him next, confirming that he was still, indeed, outside.

He moaned. "Who hit me?"

"That would be Karl," Emma replied, standing behind him somewhere. "He doesn't like you very much."

"Karl? Right, well, he's now at the top of my shit list."

"I thought I was?" Gunter asked, smiling, squatting in front of Jack.

He looked up at Gunter, blinking against the high sun. "No, I just think you're a piece of shit."

He frowned and raised his clenched fist.

"Brother, no," Emma said, "we need Jack to be with us on this little adventure."

"Better listen to Sissy, *Hans*. She's the boss, right?"

Gunter huffed an annoyed breath and stood. He stomped off and disappeared outside of Jack's limited peripheral vision.

Through a pounding headache, Jack saw that he'd been moved from the grounds just outside of Crematorium I, to the loading area at the center of the kitchen buildings. They formed a rectangular ring around a space that was currently being used as a corral for the hostages.

"Get him up."

Emma's order was answered by two people Jack had never met, and nor were any of them her team members. The pair that helped Jack to his feet were children. They sniffed and wept openly. A woman off to Jack's right was sobbing uncontrollably. She must have been their mother, and she was scared to death for her kids.

It was a no-win situation. These people's lives were in his hands. If he succeeded, maybe, just maybe, they'd be spared. Emma was dedicated, but Jack didn't think she was homicidal. She was just trying to intimidate him.

And it was succeeding.

His mind went back to his last mission with Delta—back to the young boy who blew himself up in an effort to try to kill Jack. Even after half a decade, it still haunted him. That was something you didn't forget—ever.

"Was that necessary?" Jack asked, turning and facing Emma.

She was now dressed similarly to her men, wearing a Kevlar vest over black fatigues. Emma didn't carry an HK416 or a backpack, nor did she wear a tactical face mask. The only weapon she had was a holstered pistol, most likely the one she drew and pointed at Jack back inside Crematorium I.

"It worked, didn't it?" she replied, crossing her arms.

They stepped away from the group. There had to be at least three hundred people present, plus the number of men Emma had brought with her.

"If you're wondering," she said, pointing upward to the roofs of the single-story buildings, "I have six men stationed here, plus a few others roaming the grounds. The men here only have one job. They are to contain the hostages, by any means." She faced the civilians and spoke loudly. "If you make a move that I disagree with, I give the order for them to open fire and kill as many of you as they can." She looked at Jack but still spoke to the crowd. "The only thing that will stop them is when they run out of bullets."

Jack gave her a curt nod, reading her loud and clear. If he did anything dumb, the blood was on his hands too.

She went to turn, but he stopped her. "Emma?"

"What is it?"

"Which one of these assholes is Karl?"

A brutish man with greying temples snapped to attention. Sticking his chest out, he rigidly waltzed up to Jack, and got in his face, stopping within a foot of him. Then, he leaned in closer and snarled.

"I am Karl."

"Down boy," Jack said, leaning away from the black-clad gorilla.

With his wrists still bound, Jack feigned nervousness. Karl relaxed some as a result. Then, Jack launched himself forward and hammered Karl in the face with his forehead. He happily watched the man collapse to the ground while holding his bloodied, broken nose.

"I said, *down*."

Gunter's face scrunched up, and he took a step toward Jack.

"Enough!" Emma shouted, drawing her pistol.

She pointed it at the closest person to her, one of the children that had helped Jack to his feet. The girl couldn't have been more than thirteen. The sight of the gun was too much, and she screeched into the air and ran. She was almost back to her mother when one of Emma's men caught her arm and threw her to the ground at Jack's feet.

He looked into the girl's green eyes.

"Hey," he said softly, "you're going to be okay."

Sniffing, she nodded and wiped her eyes.

Jaw tight, Jack returned his attention to Emma. "So, when do we get started?"

4

Gunter and the man Jack headbutted, Karl, forcefully ushered him along behind Emma. Two other men with assault rifles brought up the rear of the group. It seemed that the expedition team was to consist of himself and five members of the modern-day *SS*. Sooner or later, Jack would need to even out the five-to-one odds.

He'd never admit it out loud, but Jack needed to see this thing through. He wanted to see if there was gold at the end of this blood-stained rainbow. The fact that the descendants of a prominent Nazi had come out of the woodwork like this told him that, at least, *they* thought it was real. That they chose Auschwitz to begin their search, and not the Owl Mountains, further intrigued him.

So far, no one had been killed. He'd "gladly" go along until something changed. He wasn't a willing participant, but if his assistance ensured that none of the hostages were murdered, then he'd play along and do his best. Wherever they were going, it was clearly some sort of undiscovered, underground entry point.

They took a right and stopped directly in front of Block 11, or as it more commonly referred to, the *Death Block*. Some of the more horrifying events had occurred within this building. Everything from sterilization experimentation, claustrophobic standing cells, and starvation torture had taken place inside the Death Block. It was one of the few places that both men and women were seen in the same light. To the doctors stationed here, they had been nothing more than lab rats or guinea pigs.

The alleyway ended at an infamous execution site, the *Black Wall*. Thousands of people had been killed by gunfire there during the war, including men, women, and even children. Most of the victims were Polish political prisoners. But as bullets ammunition became harder and harder to find, the Germans turned to alternate means of execution.

Emma headed right and continued up a short flight of steps,

pausing just outside of the Death Block entrance. She turned and unzipped her Kevlar vest. Emma reached in and procured a worn, leather bound book. Flipping it open, she carefully thumbed through the pages, translating its contents to herself. All Jack could do was stand there and watch her mouth silently open and close.

Finally, Jack had to know.

"What's that?" he asked, tilting his chin toward the book.

Emma didn't look up. "Himmler's journal."

Jack was blown away. "That belonged to Heinrich Himmler?"

She glanced up at him. "It did, but I've had it in my possession for some time now. I know it by heart. Himmler sent it to my great-grandfather before going into hiding."

"And it'll help us how, exactly?"

She slid it back into her vest and zippered it shut. Standing erect, she explained.

"Himmler knew that someday Hitler's reign would end, and with it, his collection would be there for the taking."

"His collection? You mean the train?"

"*Ja.*"

"So," Jack continued, "you think the entrance to some hidden tunnel system is inside the Death Block?"

Emma smiled. "No," she turned and entered the popular tourist attraction, "not exactly."

Oookay.

Gunter ordered one of the men to stay put outside the door. Jack's chances of survival had just gone up. Now, his odds were four-to-one.

He was shoved along behind her. As they moved indoors and out of the public eye, the four gunmen ditched their tactical masks, opting for a more comfortable approach. Gunter kept him moving with the help of a pistol. Emma continued down the steps into the basement level, the Cellars. This was where some of the most abhorrent tortures had occurred at the hands of Nazi scientists and physicians.

It'd make sense to hide a secret access point down here. It was said that some of the soldiers that had been stationed at Auschwitz didn't have the stomach to step foot in the Cellars. Even now, decades later, the place gave Jack the chills. Emma stopped and turned again, once more producing the Himmler journal.

She thumbed it open and stopped at a middle page.

"Himmler didn't want just anyone to find the train, so he left somewhat cryptic clues for a worthy person to follow. For instance, it starts with 'Death is absolute. No one is above death.'"

Jack looked up at the ceiling, visualizing the building he stood in. "The lower levels of the Death Block."

She nodded. "Very good. Not terribly difficult, but still, he didn't just give it away. He made sure that the reader would have to be on-site to understand it properly. Plus, the bunker would be easiest to defend if he were forced to fall back." She smiled. "And so would the secret."

"Not if the Allies had done what they should've and bombed the shit out of this place once it was emptied," Jack said. There were very few places of immense historical value that he wished had been wiped off the map in their heyday. Auschwitz was one of them. "Oh, and this doesn't feel very secretive. Feels kinda lazy, if you ask me. What's the next 'clue?'"

The jab at Himmler, a man that Emma obviously admired, caused her face to tighten. With a clenched jaw, she said, "Iron will lead you to your destiny."

Jack stretched his back and shoulders the best he could while he took in the corridor. To his right was a secondary hallway that held a series of isolation chambers. On his left was a similar passage. It housed the suffocating standing cells.

Further down the corridor, past Emma, was one of three gates, but there was only one that was locked. Jack's tour guide, Kasper, had said that the only thing beyond it was a series of offices that were dilapidated and too dangerous for visitors to enter. There had been an attempt to rebuild them at one time, but the long-time director of the museum canceled the restoration for fear of doing more harm than good to the rest of the building.

"Hmmm," Jack muttered, thinking.

"Yes?" Emma asked.

"The gate behind you is locked, and I'm pretty sure it's made of iron."

She turned and looked, mumbling something in German. Another of the other mercenaries handed Karl his carbine and quickly removed his backpack. He removed a blowtorch and moved off with Gunter in tow. The two men swiftly went about cutting through the antique partition. Jack was left alone with only Emma and Karl. The latter's face was a mess. His nose was swollen, and both of his eyes had already started to bruise.

Jack winked. "Lookin' good, my friend."

He knew Karl wanted nothing more than to beat him to death, but they needed him. Keeping the guy annoyed was not only amusing, but it was also part of Jack's plan. It'd keep at least one of Emma's goons off-center and more susceptible to mistakes. That's what Jack hoped, anyway.

Something about this whole thing bothered Jack—besides the zip-cuffs, guns, and Nazi militants. The clues Himmler left behind were simple. Emma should've been able to figure this out without him. It begged the question...

Why am I here? Jack asked himself. The only thing he could think of, besides being a hostage, was something even more terrible, like a boobytrap of some kind. Not that he was complaining, in the least. They could've simply put a bullet in his head and left him to rot inside the crematorium.

So, he watched and waited for the real challenge to show its ugly mug. Something awaited them—something that Emma wanted him, not one of her men, to take head-on.

"Yay, me," he mumbled under his breath. Karl overheard him and glared at him. Jack smiled. "I'm just super honored to be here."

The brute rolled his eyes and shoved Jack forward at the shriek of a gate swinging open. The cry of metal made the group cringe, reverberating through the tight confines of the concrete Cellar walls as well as everyone's spines.

Jack glanced at Karl. "Like nails on a chalkboard, huh?"

Karl growled and pushed Jack, causing him to stumble through the heavy iron gate and into the wall at the end of the T-junction. Grabbing Jack's shirt, Karl pinned him there, drew his sidearm, and jammed the barrel into his temple.

"Keep talking, funny man, and I'll take you outside and give you an up-close look at the Black Wall."

"Karl!" Emma shouted, standing outside one of the four doorways. Two of the offices were to Jack's right, where Emma stood now. Two others sat to his left. All of them were situated against the western wall.

"It's this one."

"How do you know?" Jack asked, joining Emma at the end of the short hallway.

There, she tapped the wooden door frame above their heads. Jack recognized the carvings. They were "mystic" Armanen runes, an alphabet based on the much older Scandinavian variation. It was partially adopted by Himmler, a member of the Thule Society of occultists, into the Nazi party. Accompanying the runes were a pair of stylized lightning bolts, the symbol of the SS.

Friggin' nutjob...

Jack glanced at the door to his left. It didn't have any markings at all. He counted to six Mississippi, and still, nothing. Emma was off somewhere else, mentally.

Jack cleared his throat. "Okay, so, why don't you pretend I'm not an expert in Armanen Runes, and tell me what it says?"

He considered himself a highly skilled "Jack" of all trades. The only expertise he truthfully had was in modern warfare. He was well-versed in many things when it came to history, but was a little fuzzy when it came to Armanen runes.

"It says, 'destiny.'"

Jack recited Himmler's clue. "Iron will lead you to destiny."

"The entrance is here," Emma whispered, lost in the moment. She blinked, refocused, and stepped in.

Jack joined her, his wrists aching. The thick zip ties had started to saw into his flesh. With every movement, they dug deeper and deeper into his skin. It was only a matter of time until they bled. He needed to remove them before then.

The room was bigger than he figured it would be, maybe twenty-feet-deep by thirty-feet-wide, and it was empty save for a large, solid-looking table pushed up against the northern, right-hand wall. *Hmmm.* The office space extended further than the rest of the building above their heads. The far wall ran under the alleyway outside. Jack took the time to inspect the room, floor to ceiling, visualizing where the wall should've ended.

He stepped up to the table and nudged it with his hip, but it didn't budge an inch. *Geez...* He stepped back and examined it further. *Is it attached?* The back of the tabletop was perfectly flush against the wall—*too* flush.

"Hey, Hans!" Jack called.

With a sour look on his face, Emma's brother joined them, gun in hand. "*Ja?*"

Jack tapped one of the front legs of the table with the toe of his boot.

"Try to move this thing, will ya?"

Gunter's right eyebrow rose, and he looked at his sister.

"Do it," she said.

Gunter shrugged and holstered his pistol. In turn, Emma redrew hers. The German pulled at the piece of furniture as hard as he could, and even still, it didn't move.

Hmmm. The add-on and table didn't make sense.

"Why build an arbitrary space such as this?" Emma asked.

"Then secure a table to it," Jack added. "Does the Himmler journal say anything about this?"

Emma faced the table and shook her head, running her hand across its surface. "None of this makes any sense." She looked back up at Jack. "Unless..."

Together, they got to their knees and inspected the underside of the desk. The first thing Jack noticed was that it was, indeed, bolted to the wall. It still didn't make any sense, though. The only time you fastened something like this to a wall was if it was in danger of tipping over, like Jack's overpacked bookshelf, back home in Wyoming.

Emma dropped to the ground and rolled onto her back. Jack would've done the same, but his bound hands said otherwise. As soon as she was on the floor, her eyes lit up.

"You need to see this."

Jack snorted out a laugh. "Then, *you need* to cut these damn cuffs off."

Emma didn't respond. She slid her phone out of her pocket and took a picture. She climbed out and knelt next to Jack, smelling wonderful. Jack took his eyes off the stunning woman and focused on her iPhone's screen instead. He was confused by what he saw.

"A padlock?"

She nodded. "Skillfully installed directly into the underside of the table."

Jack stood and inspected the tabletop and saw no hint of the lock on the other side.

"But we have no key," Gunter said.

Shit, Jack thought. *Now what?*

Emma's eyes lit up. "But I know who does!"

5

Ten minutes ago, Jurgen, Karl's partner, and Jack's other prison guard, had left to find Emma's mystery person. Whoever it was, they were here, and he, or she, supposedly owned a key that fit into their equally mysterious lock.

Jack made himself at home and climbed onto the wall-mounted table. It's where he sat until an older man inched his way inside. The newcomer saw Jack defiling the relic and gasped in horror. It was clear to see who he was, even if Emma didn't introduce him.

"Jack Reilly," she said, "I'd like you to meet, Piotr Symanski. He's been the director of the Auschwitz-Birkenau State Museum for nearly four decades..." she gave Jack a predatory smile, "and a Nazi sympathizer for even longer."

"Charming," Jack said, swinging his legs like a child.

"Does he have to sit there?" Piotr asked.

Jack shrugged. "I'd move to a chair, but you didn't leave any out." He pouted. "You're a real shitty host, Pete."

Piotr seemed to have the same sense of humor as Emma and her troops. That's to say—none. Still, Jack waited for Emma to explain why the closeted Nazi was gracing them with his presence.

"Tell them," Emma said.

Piotr nodded. "My father was a man named Klaus Wagner, and during the Second World War, he served as deputy commandant here at Auschwitz, a high honor. He was also the cousin of the camp's first commandant."

"Hang on, your father knew about this place?"

Piotr's face softened. "He did, but my mother burned everything of his after he left us. As you can imagine, she wasn't very happy with him up and leaving. It wasn't until she passed away that I found a key in her safety deposit box. She never once mentioned its existence."

Humanity dodged a bullet there. Jack appreciated Mrs. Symanski's rage-fueled response to her husband walking out on his family. She had inadvertently saved mankind from Piotr, or anyone else, for that matter, from finding the train.

"Your lineage is just as terrible as Emma and Gunter's," Jack said.

Piotr's eyes narrowed. "Says the American whose government sticks their noses in everyone else's business."

Jack wasn't about to get into a political debate right now. So, he did the smart thing and silently shrugged his shoulders. He let the man have his small victory if only to keep him talking. Jack needed to know everything. Knowledge was power in this case. The more Jack knew, the more useful he'd stay.

"So," Jack said, "how is it that no one has found out about you after all of these years? I figured a man of your stature would've been back-checked thoroughly."

He smiled. "Who says that I haven't been?"

Right, like Emma, there were still plenty of those that followed and believed in the old ways. It shouldn't have shocked him that a person like Piotr would be one of them. Who knew how many were hiding inside the world's governments? There could be thousands— millions—of them waiting for someone like Emma to emerge and lead them to conquest.

"And the lock?" Jack asked.

Piotr grinned, showing off a set of yellowed teeth. "It requires a key." Carefully, he removed a necklace from around his neck. At the end of the simple knotted cord was an iron key. "After my father vanished, my mother and I fled to Austria. We changed our names and started over as refugees."

Emma explained their relationship. "When I discovered who Piotr was, we formed a bond."

"What's your cut?" Jack asked, eyeing the man. This wasn't only a noble endeavor. Piotr also wanted to get rich.

"One percent," the director answered.

One percent of thirty billion dollars was a lot of money. Jack could only imagine what he'd do with the three hundred million that Piotr was promised. In the museum director's case, he'd probably leave it to his existing family and donate a portion of it to his and Emma's cause.

"And yours?" the museum director asked.

Jack laughed. "Oh, man, Pete, you must also moonlight as a stand-up comedian!" His eyes flicked to Emma. "You think I'm willingly helping this scum?"

"Watch yourself, Jack," she warned, raising her gun.

Jack didn't flinch. Instead, he just rolled his eyes and hopped off the table. "Come on, Pete, let's get this over with."

He nervously handed over the family heirloom to Emma, and she did the honors.

"Why haven't you done this already?" Jack asked. Piotr had the key in his possession this entire time.

Emma sighed and pushed past Jack. She got down on her knees and rolled onto her back again. "Sadly," she explained, "we would've approached him long ago had we know who he really was."

"And you?" Jack asked, looking at Piotr.

"I have no way of doing this on my own at my advanced age. And until now, I didn't know who to trust."

Careful what you wish for, Pete. Jack suspected that there were few people Emma wouldn't kill if she felt the need to.

There was a beat of silence in between Emma and Piotr's explanations. Then, a *clunk* resounded from somewhere behind the wall. Even after everything Jack had been through, the hair on the back of his neck stood on end. He was excited to see what happened next.

Emma climbed out from under the table and stood next to Jack. Gunter stepped up next to him as well. Like his sister's eye, his were also bursting with excitement. Piotr had yet to move again since handing over his key. Even now, he stood hunched, nervously fiddling with the keyless cord. Karl and Jurgen, who had remained outside the room the entire time, had since moved to the doorway. Everyone was curious as to what would happen next.

Nothing.

"Um," Jack said, looking around.

But then, barely above a whisper, he heard it. There was a muffled clicking somewhere behind the wall. It reminded Jack of a kitchen timer buried beneath a pile of pillows. He skirted around the table and placed his left ear and shoulder against the wall. Leaning in, he pressed himself as flat as possible and listened.

Without warning, the section of wall in front of him dropped straight down into the floor. Thrown off-balance, Jack spilled to the floor of a hidden room. Except he didn't hit it. Along with a rush of air, Jack continued down a set of spiraling metal stairs. He went round and round for what felt like minutes. Jack had no idea which way was up, nor how deep he was traveling. Eventually, the battered and bruised park ranger came to an abrupt halt, landing flat on his chest on a hard, dusty, concrete floor.

Everything had happened so quickly that he didn't see what else, if anything, was behind the false partition. Regardless, the Nazis had built a secret passageway beneath Auschwitz. It connected to what must've been some sort of natural cave system. The area around him was too dark to confirm his theory. And all he cared about now was catching his breath and waiting for the pain to subside.

Jack stayed put until he heard the banging footfalls of his captors closing in. Moaning, he gingerly rolled onto his side and tried to get a better look at where he was. All he saw was the aura of a flashlight as it came down from heaven to greet him. Emma was the first to appear. Then her brother, who was closely followed by Karl and Jurgen.

None of them moved to help Jack.

The foursome conversed amongst themselves in German while shining each of their lights around the room. Jack figured its size was reasonably significant since they sounded excited about what they saw—like, a Victoria's Secret BOGO sale kind of excitement. He'd read about Nazi bunkers being found all over German-occupied Europe.

As part of his plan to foil an Allied invasion, Hitler commissioned army engineers, as well as Dutch slave laborers, to build a line of covert bunkers. They were known as the "String of Pearls." It was an arm of his Atlantic Wall that reached from the Netherlands all the way to the Bay of Biscay in France, nearly 1,000 miles in distance.

Jack turned and watched as Emma hugged Gunter. The two were ecstatic about something Jack couldn't see yet, and it pissed him off.

"Hey...a little help here?"

Emma didn't verbally answer. She just motioned to Jack, and Karl and Jurgen did as directed. He was lifted roughly off the ground, placed on his feet, and was then let go without making sure he could stand on his own. Luckily, Jack didn't feel anything broken, though he hurt in several places—too many to count.

His worst injury was to his head. Jack felt warm liquid slowly making its way down his right temple. Again, no one in Emma's group gave a damn about what condition he was in. They were wholly absorbed in the space behind Jack. So, he turned and almost fell over by what he saw.

He did his best Jackie Gleason impression and said, "Well, sumbitch." It was a good representation of his character from *Smoky and the Bandit*. He would've made Sheriff Buford T. Justice proud.

Thanks to the beams of four high-powered LED flashlights, he saw an underground World War II-era community. The engineering on display was incredible. It screamed of a nuclear fallout shelter. In front of him was a workstation consumed entirely of communications equipment. In total, the room was thirty feet squared, and...it wasn't the only one.

It reminded him of the video game, *Fallout 4*.

To Jack's left and right were additional living and working quarters. The *Vault,* as the game called them, held more rooms straight ahead, for as far as the flashlights could reach. In all, there may have been a dozen rooms of similar size hiding directly beneath Auschwitz. Jack was aware that escape tunnels under Auschwitz had been found in the past, but nothing like the size of this bunker had ever been reported. It was evident that Hitler had been preparing for some of his higher-ups to disappear underground and go into hiding for an extended period.

"Over here," Jack said, limping to the doorway on their left.

Only Karl joined him. *Great.* He did give Jack some much-needed light, though. Jack peeked in and saw a full-sized kitchen and living room complete with a smoke vent and electricity. The still-packaged food and equipment stacked in the corner of the room also confirmed Jack's hypothesis that they had planned to be down here for quite a while, maybe even long after the war had ended.

"Look at this," Emma said, standing in the doorway to the right of the entry point.

With nothing else to see in his room, Jack joined her, as did the others.

The area beyond was jam-packed with weapons of all kinds. Dozens of chests and crates lined every available inch of wall space and most of the interior of the room too. It seemed that the plan had been to re-emerge with gusto after their stay underground was complete. It was obvious that they had planned on killing a lot more people.

6

Emma and Gunter entered the weapons cache first, eager and flabbergasted. It was precisely how Jack used to react to seeing a mountain of presents on Christmas morning as a child. The awestruck look on the siblings' faces was understandable, in a way. Even Jack was impressed with the find. They had just discovered a long-forgotten Nazi stronghold, something the historical community would drool over for years. Everything was perfectly preserved and in near-mint condition too.

He recalled the gust of air that flowed around him when he fell down the stairs. The bunker was somehow pressurized, lacking any oxygen at all. It had helped preserve everything inside the underground sanctuary.

Large metal boxes were situated around the "weapons locker" with tight passages in between the inventory. There was a maze of access points. Jack picked one and decided to do some reconnaissance while still shaking off his fall. He strolled down the path to his left under the ever-watchful eye of Karl. Jack wasn't going anywhere, though. He was still bound and had no way of safely navigating the dark confines of the bunker.

Jack smiled. He had chosen the correct path. On a table in the corner of the room was a bevy of run-of-the-mill German trench knives. Each would fetch a pretty penny on the private market, but they'd also be an excellent way for Jack to defend himself.

He made no sudden moves. Instead, he turned his back to the assortment and found Karl. The larger man was staring him down but couldn't see what he was doing behind his back. Smooth and easy, Jack wrapped his fingers around the first knife he could find and moved off, slowly working it up into his jacket's right sleeve. While he worked to conceal his find, he pretended to inspect something else. He'd attempt to cut himself free later. Either way, he now had something better than his forehead to use as a weapon.

In the auras of the other flashlights, Jack noticed an opening to his left. He inched closer and saw something he didn't like. There, on the floor of the next room, was a boot. And It was attached to someone.

"Over here," Jack said, motioning with his head for Emma to join him.

She did and pointed her light his way. Three steps later, the beam paused on the ground beyond Jack. Emma whispered something to her team, and they all gathered around the discovery. Unsurprisingly, it was the preserved remains of a German soldier. The man's dated uniform confirmed that he'd been down here since World War II.

But how long after?

Could there have been a community of Nazis living beneath Auschwitz in the years following the war? If so, for how long? The first room, the one with the communications equipment, didn't shed much light on the answer, but if they had been down here for months, or possibly even years, the rooms should've shown more signs of activity. Nothing, not even the food, had been unpacked.

No, Jack didn't believe that. This man's presence was an anomaly. He wasn't supposed to be here.

Emma's light focused on his nametag and then his face. They all instantly knew what had happened. The hole in his forehead made it evident.

"He was executed," Jack said, trying to work it out. "Why?"

"The Allies must've known of this place," Gunter said.

"No," Jack said, "that doesn't make sense. If they did, they would've cleared this place out shortly after finding it." He tipped his chin to the body. "The weapons, and our friend here, would've been moved."

He glanced at Emma, who took a deep breath and sighed. Like Jack, she had already figured it out. "He was betrayed."

"By who?" Gunter asked, kneeling beside his political ancestor.

"Best guess..." Jack said. "Probably by someone who didn't want this place to be found."

Emma cautiously stepped through the doorway. "The killer had known what was down here and silenced anyone who knew of its location."

Gunter grunted and stood. "Which means, we'll find more bodies."

Jack wasn't sure of anything yet, but sure, he'd go with that until proven otherwise. Okay, so maybe there was a horde of treasure down here, or near here, at the very least. But Jack seriously doubted that there was anything remotely as big as a covert train station beneath Auschwitz.

Yet, here he was, in a top-secret Nazi bunker.

"How deep do you think we are?" Jack asked.

Emma shrugged. "I'd say we're at least sixty feet beneath the Cellar's lower level."

I agree.

Jack felt like he'd just fallen down six stories worth of hard, metal stairs. Still...

"How has this place never been found?"

"Auschwitz sits atop it," Emma said. "Besides that, Oswiecim doesn't offer much else to the world besides a historic lookback."

"It's a small town," Gunter added. "Less than forty thousand residents. It's very old, but other than that, there isn't much to see."

Right, Jack thought, *the perfect place to hide something like this.*

Only World War II history buffs would care. And those looking for the gold train were busy looking for it 125 miles away in the Owl Mountains. Plus, in Piotr, Auschwitz had a Nazi sympathizer running the place. Then, enter in someone with the knowledge of the Schmidts. It was the perfect storm.

With nothing else to see here, Jack followed Emma into the next room. It was twice the size of the weapons locker and held three rows of metal-framed bunk beds. By Jack's count, the living quarters were designed to sleep seventy-two people.

He inspected the first set of bunks and noticed that a footlocker sat at each end—one for each resident. With the tip of his boot, Jack lifted the lid of one of them. Inside were someone's tightly packed personal effects. It appeared that this person was never given a chance to move in but had been ready to. Jack glanced over his shoulder at the body.

Seventy-two men, he thought. He replayed Gunter's words in his head.

"I think you might be right," Jack said, eyeing Emma's brother. The siblings joined Jack and were taken aback by what he found. "I think we're gonna find more bodies."

"What?" Emma said, lifting a   framed picture out of the locker. It showed a family. They were happily posed together in the middle of some unknown park. A man dressed in German Army fatigues stood proudly next to what must've been his wife. There were also three young children present.

Gunter lifted the lid of another locker. It was like the one before, full of clothes and intimate belongings. Some even held handwritten letters. With a shaking hand, Emma carefully removed one and opened it, reading it to herself.

Once she finished, tears streaked down her typically stoic face.

"This man..." she explained, regaining her composure. "He left his family behind to follow the *Fuhrer.*" She looked at Gunter—her own flesh and blood. "He abandoned his wife and children to be here." She wiped her eyes, looking embarrassed by the show of emotion. "It ends with him saying that he loves them and that he'll see them again..." Emma locked eyes with Jack, "in two years."

The bunker went silent once more.

The stillness in the dank air was haunting to Jack. In the insulated environment, the only thing he could hear was his party's breaths and their footsteps. Quietly, they exited the living quarters and headed into the next room on their left. Inside was a quaint gymnasium. Six stations of simple free weights dotted the space. Seeing nothing of real interest, Jack and Emma led the group through the next doorway.

"A theater?" Jack asked, spotting the old-timey projector near the back of the room.

Ten simple folding chairs were set up facing a blank wall. It appeared as if the gift of entertainment would've been part of the lengthy stay.

"Movies?" Gunter asked.

"To keep morale high," Jack explained. "Imagine how wound up people like this could get without a way to relax."

Karl stepped forward. "What do you mean, 'people like this?'"

Jack shrugged. "You know, Nazis? Filth..."

"Let's go," Emma said, not paying attention to Jack and Karl's banter. Jack hustled along before Karl could physically retaliate, and he followed closely behind the Schmidts.

There wasn't much of anything inside, except for a submarine-style hatch on the rear wall. Jack was unable to help the others open it. But Karl and Jurgen, with their combined strength, managed to get the circular wheel going. After a handful of turns, the lock fully disengaged, and the two thickly built men pulled the hatch open with hardly a sound—nor was there a rush of air like before. The void beyond already contained oxygen.

As the door swung inward, Jack noticed that Emma was fiddling with something on the right-hand wall. Gunter joined her, and between them both, their bodies concealed the discovery from Jack. Patiently, he waited for them to part, and when they did, he was impressed by the ingenuity.

Bolted to the wall was an aged electrical knife switch. Jack pictured a mad scientist "throwing the switch" and powering up one of his horrible inventions. Gunter did just that. He threw the switch, and instantly, after a pop and a grind, lights bloomed to life in the next room. Somehow, the complex still had power.

Jack was the last to step through the low opening. It took a second for his eyes to adjust, and when they did, he dared not blink. The contents of the room were too incredible. Not only was space vast, but it was also deep.

"Holy shit," Jack said under his breath. "It does exist!"

7

A train station had been built into a natural spherical cave. Unfortunately, besides the platform and tracks, it stood empty. Still, the station existed. Train tracks typically meant a train was somewhere nearby. Whether it had billions of dollars in loot on it was another thing. Regardless, the station was a great historical find, more than anyone else had ever found concerning the gold train.

Directly in front of them, a steep staircase was cut into the natural sloping cave. Jack quickly started his descent, not waiting for the others. He wanted to see what else he could find before anyone else could.

As he moved, he felt the trench knife shift inside his jacket's sleeve. At some point, Jack's adventuring side needed to take a backseat to the realist side. Sooner or later, he'd need to make his escape and contact the authorities.

Halfway down the steps, Jack paused and, once more, took in his surroundings. Directly beneath his perch was a large flat slab of concrete, not unlike what a typical train station employed. But off to his left was a series of switchbacking ramps starting back up at the door they'd just entered through. The trail ended at a cluster of wheeled containers. It hit Jack. Not only was it a train station, but it was also a loading dock.

He took half a step forward but stopped when something cold struck his head. Looking up, Jack winced as a second drop hit him. This time, it was his face. The cave's roof was leaking. It had been active for quite some time. So much so, that Jack was forced to avoid a worn section of stairs. The gently dripping water had done severe damage over the years.

As far as the train tracks were concerned, they continued straight ahead into a tunnel that was noticeably man-made. There were thick wooden supports bolted into the walls, not unlike a coal mine.

Jack made it to the platform first. He was impressed to see that it was, mostly, still intact. There were only a few cracks that he could see. Emma and Gunter headed straight for the tracks that ran to the north. They stopped at the precipice and gazed over the edge, speaking in low voices. Jurgen stayed on the staircase and kept watch.

As for Karl, he only had eyes for Jack.

Jack gave the man a playful wink and headed for the discarded, four-wheeled containers. In reality, they were closer to light-weight mine cars than anything else. He slipped past the first one and worked the trench knife out of his sleeve. He immediately went about sawing into the thick black zip tie. Jack couldn't tell how far he had gotten when Emma approached him. He barely got the blade back into his sleeve before she also rounded the cart.

"Find anything?" she asked.

Jack shrugged and nervously looked around. Had she seen him?

Something to his right caught his eye. A classic, one-wheeled wheelbarrow was turned over up against the rocky cave wall. But it wasn't the wheelbarrow that got his attention. It's what was inside of it.

Emma saw it too.

Together, they headed towards it and knelt. There, inside the simple transport, was a single gold coin.

Gently, Emma reached down for the artifact, picking it up as if she expected it to turn to dust in her hand. She exhaled, hands shaking with a combination of nerves and enthusiasm. *That's one helluva cocktail!* Stamped into the coin's surface were the words Deutsches Reich, "German Reich." Accompanying the script was a symbol the Germans had used as much as the Hakenkreuz, the hooked cross, during the war. It was the Reichsadler, the imperial eagle. The eagle had often been combined with the swastika to make the formal symbol of the Nazi party.

"This is incredible," Emma said, standing.

She hurried off, shouting for the others to come over.

They did. Each one was as stunned as Emma. Even Jack. It proved that, at some point in the past, the Nazis had, undeniably, moved some of their collected wealth down here. It also confirmed that there was a train somewhere beneath Poland. What it didn't prove, however, was whether or not the transport still existed today.

It's a start, though, Jack thought.

"Look," Karl said. His face was grimmer than usual. He lifted a single finger and pointed to somewhere off the northern end of the platform.

Jack hadn't paid attention to the tight gap between the platform and the cave wall. To his left, a second, smaller tunnel headed off to who-knows-where. When Jack stepped up to the edge and took a look, it filled him with a sense of dread. Not only were there four old-fashioned mineworker's pump carts lined up there, but there was also a pile of corpses, and from what he could see, they all shared the same fate as their friend back upstairs.

Death by execution.

The hand carts did solve one problem, though. The Owl Mountains were over a hundred miles away. Jack couldn't imagine walking the entire thing under the current circumstances.

"You know," Jack said, tipping his chin toward the carts, "if we're going to use those things, you might want to cut me free."

"Do it," Gunter ordered, unhappy. He drew his pistol and stepped back.

While Jurgen cut Jack free, Gunter and Karl made sure he didn't try anything funny. Luckily for Jack, he hadn't made much progress on his own when trying to cut through his bonds. If he had, the cut marks would've tipped his captors off that he was armed.

When the zip cuffs fell away, Jack relished in his newfound freedom. It lasted all of five seconds. Gunter held up a second, thick zip tie with a grin. Rolling his eyes, Jack held out his hands and was, again, restrained. He could, at least, take solace in the fact that the extra-large zip tie was in front of him and on a different, fresher spot.

One by one, they climbed down off the platform. Jack clambered aboard the teetertotter-style cart, along with Emma and Gunter. He was forced to pump backward—not that it made much of a difference. Without a flashlight of his own, Jack couldn't see much of anything, no matter which way he faced. And, per the usual, Karl and Jurgen brought up the rear.

It took more effort to get moving than Jack would've thought. He'd never manned a handcart before, and once he felt comfortable and got into a rhythm, they were forced to stop.

Their track didn't connect with the primary line.

Gunter shouted for Karl to do something. The other man obliged without argument and jumped down from his cart. He hustled over to the railroad switch and muscled the lever over to his right. With a grind of metal, their track merged with the central one. Jack, Emma, and Gunter were already in motion before Karl got back to Jurgen.

Jack used both of his bound hands to pump up and down while Emma and Gunter only used one each. Their free hands were holding flashlights. Either he got a blinding LED beam in the face, or he saw nothing except darkness.

The track up ahead—behind Jack—wasn't in the greatest of shape, and since he couldn't see squat, he held onto the pump bar as tight as he could. They dipped and bent back and forth beneath an untold tonnage of earth. It was horrifying to think of just how much rock was above their heads.

Zoning out for what seemed like hours, he almost missed Emma and Gunter's shared expressions. Both looked unsure of what they were seeing. They slowed, which allowed Jack to check his watch. He sighed. He'd only been on the handcar for a few minutes—and, boy, was he feeling it.

The Schmidts didn't communicate what they were doing, but Jack felt the pair ease up on their half of the pump bar. So, he did the same, turning and looking behind him as they slowed. He instantly found what concerned the siblings. A massive pile of rocks blocked their path. At some point between now and the Second World War, the tunnel had caved in and crushed the tracks.

They came to a full stop fifty yards shy of it.

Jack didn't get down right away. He wanted to see what they were going to do first. The fingers of his left hand slid into the right sleeve of his jacket, just in case. If this was the end of their journey, Emma and Gunter could quickly cut bait and retreat to the surface, which meant that Jack was expendable.

He—the hostage—needed to keep himself relevant.

Before anyone forced him off, he hopped down and took a look around. With his hands in front of him now, he was able to itch his nose, a feat that was only possible beforehand if he used his shoulder. The boulders laying atop the track were enormous. A few were taller than he was. There was no way they'd be able to move them, even if they cut Jack's wrists free again.

Jurgen called out from somewhere behind them. He spoke in German, which meant that Jack had no idea what the hell he was saying. The private conversations were quickly getting on Jack's nerves. Gunter replied and looked at Emma. She, thankfully, remembered that Jack didn't speak the language and quickly translated.

"He says that he spotted an outlet a hundred yards back the other way."

"So," Jack said, "we're going off the reservation?"

Emma looked unsure, but she nodded. "*Ja.*"

"Can I at least have a flashlight?"

Without turning, she called for Jurgen. In rapid-fire succession, she told the man to do something. The mercenary wasn't thrilled, which meant it was probably a good thing for Jack. He unslung his pack and produced a small black Mini Maglite, handing it over with a scowl. Jack clicked it on and smiled. He, now, had the gift of sight.

"Okay, Jack," Emma said, stepping aside. "Lead the way."

"Really?" he asked, not trusting her.

She stepped up next to her brother. "Better something terrible happens to you than us."

"Yes, my lady," he announced, "I shall be your shield."

Jack headed back the way they'd come, feeling the trench knife in his sleeve. He stepped around the pair of handcarts, looking them over as he did. Jack was impressed that they worked as well as they did. His shoulders fell. He wouldn't be able to operate one on his own if he was able to make a break for it. Maybe if they were brand-new and their gears freshly oiled, he'd be able to, but not now.

He was just about to suggest using the handcarts but stopped outside a small passageway. He sighed. Looking it over, Jack saw that the track leading inside was in good shape, but the railroad switch wasn't. The pole attached to the gearbox had been severed at the base. There was no way to throw it in their favor.

Being cautious with his footing, Jack slowly crept into the offshoot. The path had originally been a natural fissure that had since been expanded by force. There would've barely been enough room to fit the handcarts through.

Behind him, Emma and Gunter quickly conversed with one another. Jack paid them no attention and focused on the task at hand. One by one, he silently counted off the number of railroad ties that passed beneath him. Jack couldn't recall where he'd read it, but he knew there were roughly 3,250 wooden beams per mile of track.

God, I hope there isn't that many.

8

After two and a half miles worth of twisting railroad ties, Jack stopped counting. There was no way to tell where they were, but they certainly weren't under Auschwitz anymore. He didn't know the area outside the complex well enough to try and figure it out either.

The passage opened ahead, rapidly relieving some of Jack's amassed anxiety. He wasn't claustrophobic—not at all—but just being in the tight confines of a Nazi tunnel system was discomforting, particularly with his present company.

"What's that sound?" Karl asked.

Jack heard it too. It was similar to the white noise of a crackling radio. He was pretty sure he knew its origin.

"Man, I hope I'm wrong."

"What?" Emma asked, hearing him.

Jack waved her off and kept moving.

As the shaft broadened, the ground beneath them fell away. The track didn't, though. It continued straight and true, extending out over a chasm. *Woah!* Jack was seriously impressed. Even with the others adding their light to his, he still couldn't see the other side.

The air around Jack was wet, like a chilly night before a storm. Every surface was covered in a layer of moisture.

Careful not to slip, Jack inched out onto the elevated track a few feet and looked straight down between the ties. He pointed his flashlight in the same direction, dreading what he saw. The moisture's origin was six stories beneath him. There, a trio of raging subterranean rivers joined as one. One flowed from directly beneath his feet. The other two were expelled from tunnels to his left and right. Together, they rushed straight under the track with all the might that the natural world could muster.

It was equal parts power and peace. Jack loved the sound of rainstorms and trickling streams. Even a raging river, such as this, could put Jack to sleep in minutes.

A nap sounded terrific right about now.

All of his appreciation for the powerful current faded as he followed the combination of tributaries. The imposing display ended at a waterfall that fell away into an even deeper darkness.

Seeing enough, Jack backed away and bumped into something dense and immovable. He turned and found Gunter staring at him with the slightest of grins on his face. Karl and Jurgen stood on either side of the German.

Jack shrugged. "What?"

Gunter finally spoke up. "Keep moving."

His words made Jack laugh. "You're kidding, right?"

"No, Jack, he's not," Emma said, stepping around the trio.

Jack glanced back and forth between the foursome. Neither of them backed down. They were dead serious, and Jack couldn't believe it. Then again, it wasn't their lives they were gambling with. It was his.

"Fine," Jack said, frustrated, "but if I die, I'm coming back as a ghost and haunting the shit out of all of you."

With extreme caution, Jack stepped toward the precipice. Since he was the guinea pig, he took his damn time and inspected the path. The train track sat atop a series of horribly rusted metal supports. The moisture had done a number on them over the years.

Slowly, Jack inched out, using the warped railroad ties as stepstones. So far, it felt stable enough. The only sound other than the rushing water was his footfalls. After twenty railroad ties in, he found one that shifted beneath him. It didn't wiggle much, but it was enough to spook him. He stopped and took a moment to collect himself.

"Oh, Jaaack," Emma called out. "We don't have all day."

Annoyed, he glanced over his shoulder. "Wanna switch spots?" She crossed her arms and glared at him. "Is that a no?" He turned around, examining his next step. "Then do me a favor, and keep that shit to yourself."

Jack headed off before the peanut gallery could speak up again. It felt good to shut them up. What didn't feel satisfying, was the track beneath his feet giving out. Surrounded by crumpling mass of steel and wood, Jack fell and plummeted into the bitterly cold water below.

Quickly swept away, Jack did two things as he was forced underwater. He gripped onto his flashlight as hard as he could, and he curled himself into a ball, tucking his chin into his chest. Much like his tumble down the stairs beneath the Cellar, Jack was battered, thrashed hard by the current. As expected, the stone walls didn't give an inch.

Suddenly, Jack was thrown from the water, freefalling again. In the aura of his flashlight, he saw that he wasn't, technically, thrown anywhere. Jack had found the waterfall. A heartbeat later, he plunged back into the river.

He managed to surface and took in two lungfuls of air just as his head nearly struck the sharply descending ceiling. Jack was comfortable in the water, but this was ridiculous. He held his flashlight out in front of him and kicked, occasionally flipping the beam up. If the ceiling didn't rise soon, Jack was going to drown. He couldn't let that happen.

He was keen on kicking some Nazi ass.

Lungs on fire, Jack pumped his legs hard, kicking like the world's most awkward frog. He had no idea how much distance he covered between his and the water's efforts, but it felt like a lot.

The current died down to almost nothing—which meant Jack was on his own. He panicked, and reflexively tried to surface, expecting to smack his head against stone. Surprisingly, he found air instead. Kicking in place, he sucked in one greedy lungful of oxygen after the other. In the half-submerged beam of his flashlight, he saw shore up ahead. Slowly, he propelled himself toward it, clumsily climbing out of the water and collapsing to the chilling stone floor. He was waterlogged and cold—two things that didn't complement one another.

If he were back in Yellowstone, he'd simply build a fire. Jack doubted there was anything to burn down here, though. Come to think of it, he had no idea where *here* was. Jack was miles outside of Auschwitz's perimeter fence by now. Until he was told otherwise, he'd assume he was traveling northwest toward the Owl Mountains. That was his best guess.

Before he did anything else, Jack stuck the end of his flashlight in his mouth and swiftly worked the trench knife from his jacket sleeve. With a flick of his wrist, he cut through his bonds and chucked them in the water.

Jack sat up and placed the small Maglite on the ground, pointing it back toward the water. There was nothing except a calm, serene pool. It was flat and glassy, beautiful even. On his hands and knees, he crawled to the water's edge and gratefully dipped his sore wrists beneath the icy surface.

Then, he scooped a few handfuls of water into his mouth. Satisfied, he kept both his hands under the water and closed his eyes, relishing in the relaxing stillness the cavern provided. He knew he should get up and try to find a way out, but instead, he took an extra moment to reset and recharge.

When he got to the point to where he couldn't feel his fingers, he removed his hands from the water and gingerly climbed to his feet, snagging his flashlight as he did. Like the floor back up by the railroad track, the one beneath his feet now was worn and slick. Jack backed away from it, wanting nothing more than to camp out for a while and rest. He knew he couldn't, so he turned and started walking away.

Jack cracked his neck and groaned. "What a day...."

He only made it one step.

Not only did Jack shiver because of the temperature, but he shook because of the wonderful discovery standing before him. He twitched with stunned excitement. Here, somewhere in a forgotten cave system within Poland's borders, was a sanctuary of stone. Straight ahead was a tall, narrow doorway cut right into the rock itself. He craned his head up and spotted a very familiar emblem carved into the wall above the entrance. It identified the owners of this place. It was simple, yet it spoke volumes. A twenty-foot, symmetrical cross adorned the arched entry.

"The Knights Templar," Jack whispered, staring up at the perfectly preserved emblem.

The Knights Templar was a Catholic military order founded in 1119. They were responsible for inventing one of the earliest forms of banking in history. They also employed some of the fiercest warriors within their ranks. Some say they left behind the greatest treasure of all.

"No way," Jack said. "It can't be..."

Was Hitler's fortune, in reality, the found Templar treasure?

It was possible. A similar organization had been in Poland during Hitler's reign.

The Teutonic Knights, also known as the "German Order," were founded decades after the Knights Templar. They acted similarly, too. They were often volunteers, but they were also paid mercenaries. Like their predecessors, the Teutonic Knights' primary goal was to assist and, if necessary, defend Christian pilgrims traveling to the Holy Land—Jerusalem. There was a small number that also took part in...extracurricular activities.

The Knights Templar were often used as shock troops during the Crusades. They were ferocious and intimidating to the enemy, exhibiting an almost otherworldly presence while on the battlefield. But unlike the Knights Templar, the Teutonic Knights' charitable arm survived into the modern era before eventually being forced underground by none other than Adolf Hitler and the Nazis in 1938.

Clandestine warrior priests. Treasure. Nazis. The connections between them all were too much for Jack to ignore.

But this place is much older than Hitler, Jack thought, panning his light over the find.

Knights Templar prayer temples could be found across Europe since before World War II. Most notably was the one recently found in Shropshire, England. The seven-hundred-year-old temple was accidentally discovered after a farmer dug up the entrance to a rabbit hole. It was an incredible story. It all started with the farmer trying to get rid of a nuisance. It ended with him finding an archaeological wonder.

Just like this, Jack thought, smiling wide.

Forgetting all about the cold, he entered the tall, elongated opening in a state of euphoric exhilaration. Its contents immediately revealed how this particular temple had been used. Lining each wall were gorgeously engraved wooden caskets. This was a secret burial chamber of the Knights Templar, and none of the coffins had been opened. It proved that Jack was the first person to lay eyes on this place in hundreds of years.

The vaulted ceilings were over twenty feet high and beautifully crafted. They showcased scenes of battle, but also images of grace. The group's history was on display here—and *he* found it! It was an amazing achievement, something he needed to share with the world.

It was just another reason that he needed to survive. Emma and her brother would undoubtedly bury the discovery after pillaging it, of course. Perhaps they'd even wipe it off the face of the earth altogether. The thought of them destroying this place sickened Jack. All of this belonged to everyone, especially the ancestors of the knights entombed here.

If he was going to tell the world about it, it meant that he needed to find a way out. He widened his light's beam and played it over the main chamber. There had to be another way out. It was inconceivable to think that the water was the only entrance.

Unless the water was a recent change? His face fell at the prospect of having the entry to the tunnel flooding over time. *Dammit.*

There was a good chance that he was trapped down here. The flooding could've occurred centuries ago. Just because the way was presently submerged, didn't mean it had always been that way.

"From a trickle to a roar." He shook his head. "No. Not happening."

Jack Reilly wasn't going out like that.

He turned and spotted a passageway, quickly entering it. He'd explore every single square inch of this place and find his damn exit. Emma, Gunter, Karl, and Jurgen—all of them—needed an uppercut to the mandible in the worst way, and Jack wanted his knuckles to do the damage.

The first corridor on his left took a hard right and then continued forever before finally ending at a blank wall. Along the way were several shallow-ish alcoves. Each was about ten feet deep, and they held nothing except a bench carved from the stone wall. They were prayer rooms. Peaceful and secluded. A perfect way to speak to God.

Feeling defeated, Jack slowly made his way back to the central chamber. Directly across the temple was another opening. He entered it and found that it was fashioned as a mirror image to the other passage. Grumbling, he stomped back to the main hall and gave it yet another look. Besides the beautiful construction, there wasn't much else to see.

"Shit." He scratched his sopping wet head. "Now what?"

Emma watched Jack plummet to what she figured was his death. She'd regret not having him along for the rest of the ride. He had proven himself to be more than valuable. She, honestly, thought she'd get a lot more out of the man.

She shrugged. "So long, Jack. It was nice while it lasted."

"It was?" Karl asked, tentatively touching his nose.

To regain their status quo, they would need to return to the surface for another hostage. It was too bad, though. Jack had been her first choice because of his knowledge. Plus, pushing around a man as skilled as him had been a thrill.

No, she decided, looking behind her. *I want my treasure first.*

After she discovered it, she'd have one of her men bring her the young girl. In memory of Jack, the girl would be Emma's new insurance policy against a counterattack.

9

Jack faced the entrance and craned his neck back, stretching it, desperately trying to knead the frustration out with both of his hands. He closed his eyes and calmed himself, taking several deep breaths. When he opened them, he noticed something about the chamber that he had missed. Along the upper half of the space was a ledge protruding no more than a foot in depth. He traced it around the room, following it until it disappeared into the rear wall. The sight made him grin from ear to ear.

There, cut into stone facing, was a black void—a doorway.

He rushed forward, through the central aisle that separated six sets of stone benches. Even they were intricately cut, right out of the cave floor. Jack ascended three stairs, stepping up onto a raised platform. Moving to the back wall, he got on his tiptoes and reached as high as he could. Unfortunately, the *podium* still wasn't quite tall enough to reach the ledge. With his flashlight back in his mouth, Jack tried, but couldn't get a good enough of a grip on the second story walkway to hoist himself up. His hands were sore, wet, and cold as hell, and the wall was too smooth to gain any purchase with his drenched shoes.

On his final attempt, he fell off the podium, nearly rolling his ankle in the process. With that, he gave up and sat in the front row.

His free hand found its worn surface, and he turned his attention to it while he took a breather. It made him happy to think that his ass was the first to grace the seat in nearly eight hundred years. The supposed timeframe was an estimate based on when the Knights Templar order had been dissolved.

"Come on, Jack," he said, looking around. "What are you missing?"

Unless the knights had brought a ladder with them to their meetings, there must've been a way up. The wall in front of him was just that—a wall. There was nothing else there besides the elevated podium. He pictured one of the group's Grand Masters going over the latest and greatest in the world of "Templaring."

The left and right walls contained the dead-ending corridors and prayer rooms, and some remarkable stone-cut artistry, but that was all. Defeated, he sighed and faced the entrance, feeling like a moron when he found what he was looking for. There, carved directly into the walls on either side of the archway, were grooves. To Jack, they kind of looked like hand and footholds.

The Templars never brought a ladder with them.

They had built one.

"Bloody brilliant," he said, slipping into a horrible Cockney accent. "Yes, yes...bloody marvelous, if I do say so myself."

Jack was exhausted, and his boyish goofiness was starting to show because of it. Few ever saw that side of him. The only one in the last half a decade that witnessed it was his partner, Bull. The guy rarely ever laughed. Jack felt so comfortable around him because of that. But it also presented him with a fun challenge.

Once, Jack even pulled out a Chris Farley impression—when Tommy Callahan butchered his father's "bull's ass" speech from *Tommy Boy*.

"No!" he muttered, flashlight in his teeth, "It's gotta be your bull."

Jack was sick of putting his Mini Maglite in his mouth. But he did it again, so he wasn't entirely without light. Taking his time, he made it a priority and kept at least three points of contact with the wall. Jack was a skilled climber. This ascent, however, was an incredibly challenging one. The thick toes of his sneakers barely fit inside the cut footholds, and he'd only just now gotten the feeling back in his fingers. But in doing so, his grip instantly improved, but so did the discomfort. The edges weren't as worn as he thought they'd be. The stone threatened to slice his skin deep as a result. He needed to take it easy and not rush.

But not too slow.

The room rumbled, and a large plume of dust kicked into the air. It only lasted a second or two, but it was enough to almost dislodge

Jack from the wall. He dug his fingertips in harder as his feet came loose. Panicked, he hurriedly kicked for purchase. When he found it, he hugged the wall until the shockwave dissipated.

"What the hell was that?" he shouted, face smushed against the wall.

Jack knew of two distinct likelihoods that could've caused the temple to shake. An earthquake was a possible origin. He had odds on an explosion, though. The people he was dealing with made the likelihood far more probable.

Jack waited a moment longer. Then, he finished the climb up to the narrow ledge. Luckily for him, he saw that it wasn't just the minute twelve inches wide he had initially estimated it to be. The shelf stuck out an additional six inches in most spots. It was still going to be a treacherous journey to the other end of the chamber.

"You made it this far, Jack." He did a quick calculation in his head—distance and time. "Come on, man. You can do this."

He put his back against the wall and leaned into it. He side-stepped to the right and inched his way around the rectangular space. It took him forever to get to the first corner, but once he did, he got into a solid rhythm and picked up his pace. Next was a long straight shot to the rear wall, and he happily traversed it without issue.

"There's no way they did this every time," he said, talking to himself. He glanced around the room. "Maybe they laid wooden beams across?" He imagined the temple looking like a high-ceilinged log cabin back in the day.

The last corner was a doozy, though. Part of the ledge was missing, and Jack was forced to hop sideways over a three-foot-wide gap. When he landed, more of the compromised stone came loose, and he nearly fell.

He picked up the pace and finished the nerve-racking trek before anything else bad could happen. Then, he blew out a long breath and examined the low-roofed, second story tunnel entrance. He wasn't sure what he expected, but it wasn't stairs leading deeper underground.

"Where are you guys taking me?" Jack asked, speaking to the long-deceased Templar architects.

One after the other, Jack's footfalls echoed around him. He took the descent slow and steady. He'd taken a beating up until now. Falling down another set of stairs would surely do him in. Besides the blood that still ran down his right temple, Jack was lucky to avoid any serious injuries. If it were up to him, it'd stay that way too.

"Don't get cocky, Jack."

He subconsciously counted off the steps. The final on came five minutes later. He exited the cramped passageway and entered another large chamber. This one, however, wasn't constructed for meetings and prayer. The large circular hollow was similar to the Nazi bunker in that it was most likely used as a shelter during times of war.

He guessed it was around five thousand square feet, and it contained a trio of stepped levels. Jack was currently on the lowest one. They all contained crudely built wooden tables and chairs, as well as stone-carved depressions the size of a grown man. Within each of the indentations were layers of a pale, grass-like substance.

"Hay?" Jack asked himself. He stepped into the center of the room, shining his light on every square inch of it. Then, it dawned on him. "They're beds!"

Jack had just stumbled upon a secret Templar stronghold. He wasn't a fountain of information when it came to the Knights Templar, but he knew that when Pope Clement had ordered the arrest of all Templars, including the freezing of their assets, a lot of them went underground due to fear of persecution. The papal directive led to dozens of them signing forced confessions. The papacy used those same confessions against them, and they were tortured and burned at the stake as a result. It was a dark time in history, for sure. Pope Clement even went as far as redistributing their property to those loyal to him.

"But not your treasure..." Jack mumbled, looking around. "Where did you put your big shiny booty?"

The Templars had been smart with their money, which also meant they'd been smart in the handling of it—more specifically—where they hid it. Today, a person's capital was mostly digital, but not theirs. The Templars had physical wealth, and if it was as vast as the stories alleged, their storage facility—their *vault*—must've been enormous.

"Unless Hitler and his boys found it first."

Was that the real reason you targeted Poland? His face fell. Did Hitler have an ulterior motive behind the invasion? *No, Jack decided, it can't be!*

The thought made Jack ill. If it were true, then it meant that the Nazi party had been secretly funded by the world's single largest collection of gold and antiquities. The "illness" moved into Jack's heart. He was, quite literally, heartbroken to think that's what the Templar treasure had been spent on.

Financing evil.

"No," he said, his dejection intensifying. He squeezed his fists tightly and shouted, "No!"

His voice echoed loudly in four directions. The emotional outburst helped him. It reset his mind to the situation he currently found himself in, and not the one the Templars had lived through. His biggest problem was that he was lost. There were three paths to choose from—doors number one, two, and three.

Before he decided to go anywhere, Jack needed to do something about his clothes. He was cold. It had sapped his strength and it was affecting his ability to focus. Jack was trained with how to survive in conditions such as this.

So, he gathered as much straw as possible. Touching it was surreal. A lot of it crumbled to dust—but not all of it! He hated the idea of destroying it, but the prospect of staying this cold, possibly even freezing to death, trumped any other concerns.

Next was a chair. The hay would get the fire going while the wood would keep it going.

He unsheathed his trench knife and found a loose stone on the floor across the circular chamber. Standing over the mound of hay and wood, he struck the flat stone several times with his blade until he got a spark to ignite. The ember landed in the dried-out kindling but didn't immediately catch. Jack leaned in close and blew softly, stoking the undecided flame. Finally, it caught, and Jack tossed more and more of the hay atop it.

Satisfied that it would burn for quite some time, he stripped out of his winter jacket and thermal long-sleeve shirt. He laid them out on the bed next to the fire and turned them over as the minutes passed. With time to kill, he followed the smoke to the ceiling and watched as it disappeared into a vertically cut fissure. It acted as a rudimentary ventilation system.

Jack doubted this was the first time a fire had been lit here. The room was collecting the heat too. After only a couple of minutes, the temperature of the chamber had increased dramatically. Carefully, Jack dragged over a large table and leaned into it. It held without a creak. Slowly, he sat, relaxing when it successfully held his weight. Content, Jack slipped out of his shoes and socks too.

He closed his eyes and sat in silence, clearing his mind and concentrating only on what he was going to do next.

Find Emma. Find the train. Find an exit.

Grunting, he climbed down from the tabletop, wrung out the remaining water from his clothes, and begrudgingly got dressed. His outfit was still a tad moist, but at least he was warm. He'd be fine as long as he didn't get wet again.

"And you're coming with me," he said, pocketing the palm-sized rock. Technically, he was stealing from a historical site. But even Jack would turn a blind eye if it meant he could start another fire, if needed.

One of the tunnels would surely take him north, but he had no idea which one. The Templars would've known these caves inside and out. The beds were evidence that they'd spent significant time beneath the surface, as were the worn stone benches of the temple.

Jack closed his eyes and took one deep inhalation. He blew it out slowly, emptying his lungs.

"Okay, let's start with door number one."

Determined to find the train before Emma and Gunter, Jack set off at a brisk pace, entering the tunnel on his left. The revelation that the Templar treasure may have been assimilated by the Nazis both enraged and fixated him. He wasn't a treasure hunter, but he'd do whatever was necessary to preserve it and the historical value it held. Jack's battles in the Middle East, and the adversaries he faced there, weren't very different than the enemy he fought now.

His grandmother's passion ran deep. Agatha would've gladly put her life on the line if their roles had been reversed. The same could be said about his grandfather. Like Jack, he would've wanted to do what was right. They didn't like tyrants, and neither did Jack.

If his grandparents were combined into one being, they would've been the perfect person for the situation Jack found himself in now. The honorable soldier and the spirited historian.

Jack stopped and looked deep inside himself, realizing something. He was the spitting image of both Agatha and Philip. Jack always ran towards conflict, thirsting for the fight against evil. It was an irrational way to think, but it's who Jack was. He also adored history more than he could explain. The revelation made him smile.

Jack's grandparents weren't the perfect people for the job.

He was.

His epiphany was met with a clunk of stone. Jack paused his march and looked down. Slowly, he dragged his foot back and noticed a circular depression in the floor. Within it was a likewise cylindrically cut piece of stone.

"Um."

Jack dove forward, just as an immense slab of stone crashed to the floor where he had just been standing. He rolled onto his back. His eyes were as wide as saucers. An ancient Templar security measure had almost crushed him.

"Boobytraps, really?" Breathing hard, he climbed to his feet and faced the blockade. Knocking on it, he said, "Well, I guess I'm not going back that way."

Jack inspected the enormous block. It was taller than the passage was, disappearing somewhere beyond the ceiling. There was no way through it except eroding the surface away with his fingernails for the next thousand years. So, he turned and continued onward. This time, Jack kept his light and his focus on the floor, not the past.

He heard the telltale sound of rushing water and cursed under his breath. He knew what it meant. It wasn't any different than the last time—when he had been with Emma and the others.

Further ahead, the tunnel abruptly ended at another chasm. Like the one he fell from, this one was also roughly sixty feet high—and like the last one, it also continued into a torrent of pissed off water.

"You have got to be freaking kidding me!" he shouted, rubbing his forehead with both hands. "Argh!" No matter what he did, he couldn't get the frustration, or his headache, to go away.

There was nowhere for him to go. Jack couldn't go back, but nor could he proceed. There was a thirty-foot gap between him and the other side. He spotted evidence of a rope bridge, but it had rotted out long ago. Traces of it hung beneath the opening under the second half of the tunnel. With no other options, Jack knew what he needed to do. He stepped close to the edge and recalled the second and third rivers back at the junction beneath the railroad tracks.

He looked down at his semi-dry clothes and shrugged. Then, he jumped and re-entered the ice-cold, raging rapids. Jack cringed as he was tossed back and forth against the sides of the submerged channel over and over again. The waterfall came and went in a blur. Eventually, he found himself back in the cave with the serene pool and the Templar temple.

Jack climbed out of the water and flopped onto his back.

"Well," he laughed, exhausted, "definitely not door number one."

10

Jack struggled to do so, but he successfully climbed back up to the second floor of the prayer temple. Then, he ignited another fire to re-dry his clothes and himself. Once he was somewhat dry, again, he tried the next tunnel. He took extreme caution, contemplating every step as if it were his last.

Door number two, the one directly across from the entrance, led Jack deeper underground, if that was even possible. He had no idea how far down he was. From what he could tell, all the main paths ran straight and true, a testament to the builder's abilities.

Ten minutes into the hike, the ground leveled-off some. When it did, Jack picked up on a soft, steady sound. As he neared, the white noise grew to a staticky crescendo. The upsurge in volume was incredible. Then, Jack stepped out into, yet another, immense hollow beneath the surface of the Earth.

It was a massive, vertically cut tube, not unlike an empty mission silo, and it disappeared into the darkness below. The floor and ceiling were entirely out of sight. Water flowed in from nearly every direction, pouring into the enormous conduit as if it were a natural storm drain. He inspected every surface of the tube and counted at least six cascading outlets.

His shoulders slumped when he spotted a thin staircase following along the wall of the circular chamber. But it also gave him hope. The steps started at his level. He was at the bottom of a staircase, and if he was at the bottom, then it meant that there was an exit veiled somewhere above him.

By his calculation, he'd have to pass beneath all six waterfalls. For their part, the stone steps looked slick and incredibly unsafe.

"Well," Jack said, feeling the spray smack his face, "so much for not getting wet again."

Thankfully, the two-foot-wide stairs weren't overly narrow. It made Jack's ascent go by quicker. He still took his time, though. He doubted he'd survive the fall as he had before. This was it. There was no calm pool in which to surface. There was no smooth shoreline to collapse on top of, either. A beautiful Templar temple wouldn't greet him. If Jack slipped and fell, he was dead.

The first waterfall he encountered exited the wall fifteen feet above his head. The main body of water avoided the steps entirely, but the spray didn't. Jack pulled his jacket higher and allowed it to take the brunt of the cold mist instead of his flesh.

He dragged himself across the wall as he passed beneath the deluge. The amount of water pouring into the tube was absurd and impossible to calculate accurately. He circled the tubular chasm twice, traveling below five more waterfalls before the staircase leveled-off at another opening. He turned and pointed his flashlight back down to his original entry.

It lined up perfectly with the tunnel behind him.

The Templars' direction was still sound. They cut the passages for a specific reason—to a particular location. It wasn't sheer luck that they aligned with one another. There was purpose to the design.

"Where are you going?" he asked the passage.

Jack noticed something different about this particular tunnel. He quickly widened the beam of his Mini Maglite by twisting its head. Jack gasped in response. This passage wasn't like the others at all. It was ornately carved, similar to the main chamber of the prayer temple. Beautiful pictographs showed the history of the Knights Templar. It showed them helping others while also being victorious in bloody battles.

Moving faster now, Jack set out at a hobbled jog and skidded to a stop a few minutes later, pausing just inside the tunnel's exit. He crept forward and was greeted by darkness. The only thing on the other side of the doorway was a yawning emptiness. The space beyond was pitch-black, and his flashlight did little to change that. When he went to narrow the bulb, it blinked and winked out.

"Dammit," Jack muttered, shaking it hard.

It didn't reignite. The small Maglite was dead and was now

nothing more than a tiny, useless metal stick. Still, he wasn't about to toss it aside. Jack slid it into one of the inside pockets of his jacket. Holding out his hands beside him, he took a step to his left and found the wall. Groping it blindly, he was confused when his fingertips touched something slimy.

"Ugh," he said, holding up both of his hands.

Unable to see what he had just touched, Jack used his other senses to determine what it was. He inhaled deeply and coughed. Whatever it was, it smelled dreadful. It was both thick and slick. The only thing he could think of was that it was a form of oil.

"Why would they need this?"

And then it hit him, and Jack was grateful to still have his rock and knife. He wiped his hand off on his pants and felt his way back to the source of the oil. After a pair of strikes, he watched as a single spark landed. A fireball instantly consumed it. The flame exploded upward and then shot away from Jack, following a track—a gutter of sorts—built into the wall of the cavern. The channel containing the viscous fluid was designed and implemented for a single purpose.

It was a light source.

Jack waited to react to what awaited him, as well as the ingenuity of the gutter system and the flammable oil that had stayed viable after all these years. Finally, the fire trail ended at Jack's right, on the other side of the doorway.

The naturally formed, though heavily retrofitted cavern, was the size of a concert hall, and it was overflowing with all forms of gleaming treasure. Footpaths were cut back and forth through piles of gold, precious jewels, and even marble and stone statues. They had all been separated by style and size.

The booty's transportation method sat atop a recessed track in the middle of the vast, funnel-shaped room. The lower track level allowed the six transport cars of the legendary Nazi gold train to be accessed easily from "ground level," like a typical modern-day variation. Directly behind the caboose was the tunnel leading back in the direction of Auschwitz. A second tunnel sat to Jack's left presumably led to the north.

"This is insane!"

The value of the find had been significantly underestimated at thirty billion dollars. Jack didn't know by how much, but he guessed it was maybe worth ten times the "reported" amount. Everything both the Nazis and Templars collected had been moved by one group and then the other.

Hitler's people had clearly found this "vault" and decided to add to it. However, the Nazi party fell before it could be relocated again, possibly to the Owl Mountains, as so many academics have theorized.

"How long ago?" Jack asked himself, staring in wonderment.

Did the Nazis find it before establishing Auschwitz? Maybe shortly after construction of the elaborate bunker? Regardless of when, Jack was sure that if Hitler had been able to dip into this vast fortune, the tides of the war would've swung drastically. The Nazis wouldn't have run out of funds and supplies. They may have even taken over all of Europe, including the United States' allies of France and Great Britain.

Then, who knows?

Maybe they funneled supplies to Japan to help squeeze the Soviet Union into submission. The Benito Mussolini-led Italian forces would've strengthened significantly too. The US would've had their hands full against a superpower that ranged from the Atlantic Ocean across Europe and Asia to the Pacific.

"Hitler got greedy," Jack deduced.

If the Fuhrer had started spending the cache, instead of hoarding it, they would've more than likely won the war. It was evident that they tried a late mobilization, but they hit a snag. The train was moved from the station beneath Auschwitz and then loaded here, though, something happened that stalled its movements.

Jack guessed that it was Hitler's death on April 30th, 1945. Once the guy offed himself back in Berlin, the Nazi party fell into disarray before officially surrendering on May 7th of the same year. Since then, the train and treasure's locations had been forgotten—lost to time and blood.

That was Jack's presumption.

There could've also been a sect inside the Nazis that didn't fully support Hitler as their leader. Maybe they kept all of this from him? A conspiracy within a legend that's also a piece of an older legend.

The Himmler journal showed that the SS commander had been working in secret, maybe even behind Hitler's back. The fact that he sent it to Emma's ancestor and not the Fuhrer proved as much. Perhaps it was just some sort of "plausible deniability." Have a clandestine organization down here while you did your Nazi thing up top.

Jack headed left and followed a series of descending trails through a sea of valuables. Six feet below the ring of fire were some of the larger pieces of the collection. One after the other, statues of Greek gods and goddesses meticulously carved out of both polished stone and bronze were lined up next to one another. Jack counted seven in all. They were in perfect condition except for a layer of dust that had built up over time.

The most significant piece in the room was on the other side of the cavern. It was a thirty-foot-tall stone statue of Julius Caesar. Jack had no idea how something that size made it down here. The only way that he knew of was to disassemble it and then put back together later. It's how modern-day museums moved their oversized pieces.

To his right, and piled up behind a low wooden partition, were weapons from all eras of history. Like the statues, the armaments had been beautifully preserved. He stopped next to the elaborate handle of a sword. Slowly, Jack picked it up and pulled it free of its sheath. The unblemished curved blade of the Persian scimitar was flawless, and it glowed in the orange and yellow flames of the chamber's fiery light.

He whistled in awe.

Putting it back was the right thing to do. Jack was going to, but then he heard shouts of excitement pick up from the tunnel to his right. What was worse was that the voices spoke German. Sword in hand, Jack ducked down just as Emma came sprinting into the treasure room. Gunter, Karl, and Jurgen were right behind her too. Jack was hoping at least one of the pricks would've died by now, but here he was, back to four-to-one odds.

Himmler journal in hand, Emma whooped into the air and leapt into her brother's outstretched arms. While the Schmidts gleefully embraced, Jack moved off, gripping the sword's hilt tight. He wasn't a defenseless hostage anymore.

Ironically, Jack was going on the offensive with a priceless artifact as his only means to inflict damage. He also had his trench knife as a last-ditch backup plan. His eyes flicked to the man bringing up the rear. He grinned when he saw Jurgen's HK416 in his hands.

Once Jack possessed a firearm of that *caliber*—pun intended—or even the German's sidearm, he knew his odds of surviving would skyrocket. Few were as good with a rifle or pistol as Jack, and he seriously doubted any of the mercenaries below could outgun him on his worst day. His aim was steady, and his eyesight was perfect.

With renewed vigor, Jack began developing a plan of attack.

Bring it on.

Emma couldn't believe her eyes. She'd never felt so happy in all her life. With her brother by her side, she'd found *her* train. She took in the room and realized that this was more than just Hitler's vaulted wealth.

There's too much, she thought, briskly moving toward the train. Nothing in Himmler's journal mentioned a collection like this. *And who lit the fires?*

Emma stopped in her tracks. Gunter was right beside her, carbine shoved deeply into his right shoulder.

She leaned in close to her brother and whispered, "We are not alone."

Gunter's eyes narrowed, and he headed off in search of their escapee, Jack Reilly.

Emma's job was the treasure, not people. People—how to kill them—was Gunter, Karl, and Jurgen's expertise. They were the soldiers, not her.

She turned her attention back to what she desired and was perplexed. She expected the train cars to be fully stocked, but not the rest. Plus, there were things that Hitler had never reported having. Most of what he collected was from the affluent families of the regions his armies overtook. The artifacts on display here were hundreds of years older than that.

Emma made her way to the front engine but stopped before arriving. There, on its side, was a shield that shouldn't have been there. It was shaped like an elongated, stylized, downward-facing triangle. And there, in its center, was a red cross.

"The Templars..." she said quietly, stunned. "It can't be."

Emma took off at a sprint for the train engine and swiftly scaled the metal ladder. She climbed aboard and found a single occupant lying on his stomach. The man's death had come long ago, but his uniform was still in good shape. His plain coveralls told Emma that he had been the train's conductor.

Near the body were two spent casings.

Like the soldiers they had found along the way, it appeared that this man had also been murdered. It looked like the conductor had tried to make a break for it before he was gunned down from behind.

Seeing enough, Emma returned her attention to the discovery and smiled wide. Not only had she found the gold train, but she had also unearthed the lost Templar fortune. It all made what Hitler supposedly amassed look like pocket change.

11

In some places, the three-foot-wide pathways were overrun with valuables. Sometime in the past, the barricades had broken and allowed their contents to flood forward. Staying low, Jack shuffled over a mound of gold coins similar to the one he and Emma found back at the station beneath Auschwitz. His movements were clumsy and noisy, and they drew the attention of one of Emma's men.

Jack saw the rifle barrel first and transferred the sword into his left hand. He scooped up a handful of loot with his right hand and quickly slung it sidearm, aiming for where he hoped the man's head would be. Three of the five coins found their mark, connecting with Jurgen's face. The non-lethal projectiles startled him and knocked him back. The slight delay gave Jack the time he needed to bring the sword blade up and deflect the weapon's muzzle away.

Mid-swing, Jack slipped and let go of the scimitar. He grabbed the first thing he could—Jurgen's lead arm. The two men immediately traded blows with one another, using whatever they could to harm the other. Jack caught Jurgen across the temple with a quick elbow strike and was thanked with a meaty fist to his ribs. Jack fell atop of the mercenary and tried to end it quickly with a swift jab to his windpipe.

It didn't work, though. Jurgen blocked the attempt with a swat of his hand and then landed a closed fist to Jack's face. Dazed, he stumbled back and fell into a neighboring pile of treasure.

He groaned and shook the cobwebs loose. Jurgen had hit him square in the left eye socket. It was a move that was meant to stun your opponent. It told Jack that Jurgen wasn't just some big, dumb ox with a gun. The guy knew how to fight. Leaning forward, Jack pushed away from the pile, but the added pressure on the ancient wooden barricade was enough to splinter it.

"Damn," Jack said, just as he and Jurgen were overwhelmed with a tidal wave.

The twenty-foot-high mound of books of all sizes rolled over the two men, burying them deep. Jack fell onto his hands and knees, having the wherewithal to shove himself off the ground.

One after the other, the dusty books pounded his back. He ducked his head down like he had when he was tossed around by the raging river. Pistol drawn, Jurgen took an oversized, leather bound volume to the forehead, and another to the groin. It was precisely what Jack was trying to avoid—even the shot to the nether regions.

The weight was too much, and Jack's right arm gave out. But then, the books let up, and he dug and tugged his way out of the paper tomb. It took him a few seconds to wriggle free, and when he did, he smiled.

Only feet from him was Jurgen's limp hand. It had been pinned in place, sticking straight into the air. And there, dangling from his inert forefinger, was a Glock 19 pistol. Favoring his ribs, Jack limped over and snagged the weapon, as well as a stray flashlight. Jurgen's must've been dislodged from his person before he was buried. Over to his left, Jack found his erect scimitar. It looked very much like the fabled sword in the stone.

Jack wrapped his left hand around the hilt and plucked it free, happy to see that it wasn't damaged during the most bizarre tsunami he had ever witnessed. He also gained a precious asset in the surge too. Jack also combed the area for Jurgen's HK416 but couldn't find it. The carbine, like its owner, was buried.

Regardless if he found the rifle or not, his odds had just gotten a lot better. If he could bet on himself, he would. Still, he needed to be careful. These weren't inner-city gangbangers. Emma's crew was staffed with trained professionals.

But Jack was one too.

He hustled into the next area. It was the largest one so far, and similar to the section of books, it was completely void of anything shiny. What it contained, it did so in spades. The collection of sarcophagi was eerie. It reminded him of a graveyard in a way. Most of them were from medieval times, but a few were older. Three were

Egyptian and had been left untouched and unopened. In fact, Jack noted that not a single one of the coffins had been accessed.

He would've given anything to stop and explore. The artistry on display was remarkable. Then again, no one had discovered this place since World War II. Jack was curious as to why the Nazis hadn't opened anything. When he was alive, Hitler had been anything but considerate.

His régime's war crimes had been very public and a mile long.

The vast majority of the Templar wealth was from their advanced banking system that had allowed Christian pilgrims to deposit their valuables for notes of credit. Once they arrived at their destination, all they would have to do was trade in their receipt, and the Templar "bank" made good on their agreement and repaid the value stated. They only kept a small percentage for themselves as payment for their services—a donation to their cause. It made traveling much safer. Thieves quickly became aware that the pilgrims held nothing of value and steered clear of them.

If a note wasn't claimed, whether because its owner died, or the note had been lost, and ownership couldn't be proven, the Templars kept the property as their own, merely adding to their swelling fortune. But even they couldn't hold onto it forever. Jerusalem fell to Islamic rule, and their grip on the Holy Land dwindled down to nothing. Eventually, the Templars fell out of favor with Pope Clement and King Philip IV and were stripped of everything.

Or so we thought, Jack thought.

If the Templars' prosperity had continued, they would've rapidly become the wealthiest group in all of Europe and controlled much of the world. There was no doubt that they would've retaken Jerusalem at some point. Their influence and bankroll would've seen to it. But instead, their leadership had been put on trial by the very people that encouraged their existence. They were betrayed and brutally killed off by the vile and corrupt.

Jack slid in behind a stone sarcophagus depicting a Templar knight on its lid. The man had been classically posed with his sword and shield vertically laid across his chest.

The detail in the knight's face was surreal. Even in stone, he looked alive. Jack peeked over the dead man and watched Emma pace in front of the train's engine. She was fully engrossed in the Himmler journal, reading it aloud to herself.

This was Jack's chance. If he could take her as his hostage, she'd have to ensure his safety. She was only armed with a pistol, which was currently holstered on her right thigh. He was roughly fifty yards from her, and he'd have an opening to traverse to get to her. Plus, she was nearly out of accurate pistol range. He weighed his options. He'd be an easy target to anyone keeping watch. Gunter, Karl, and maybe even Jurgen were still out there looking for him, though the latter was probably still buried in paperwork. If they observed him advancing on their leader, they'd react with violence.

Unless I get to her first, he thought, thinking it through.

Even if he did get to her before they could react, then what? Jack wasn't about to murder the woman in cold blood despite who she represented and what her goals were. He was never one to kill anyone or anything without reason. Jack wasn't soulless.

But these guys are.

He understood what may need to happen. Gun to Emma's head, Jack might be forced to pull the trigger. Mercenaries weren't loyal to anything except money, and radical ones, like Emma's men, would scatter once the snake's head was removed.

Jack made the smart decision instead of the easy one. He circled around to the rear of the train. He did so while staying within the first layer of archaeological wonders. The collection of sarcophagi ended at the tunnel from which Emma and the others had entered. For a moment, Jack thought about slipping away and heading for the surface. They had somehow made it through the blockade back near where the track split.

"Then what?" he asked himself.

No, Jack wasn't about to abandon his discovery. If he did, *they* would win.

Quietly, he climbed down onto the tracks and bypassed the exit. He pushed himself up onto the other half of the platform and rolled onto it, scrambling behind the rear car just as Gunter appeared from where Jack had been only moments earlier.

Now completely concealed, he sprinted toward the front of the train, stopping between the first and second transport cars. He spotted Emma through the gap between them. She had moved away from the engine and joined her brother further out on the other platform.

Jack needed to get closer, but he needed to do it without being seen. Traversing the couplers between cars was one option, but if he made too much noise, he'd be a sitting duck. Jack backed away from the rear of the first car and looked it over. It was different. This one was a classic passenger car, whereas the other five were solid with no windows.

He headed back to the gap between the first two cars and waited for Emma and Gunter to move away. When they did, Jack made his move for the rear door. Grasping it, he prayed it was unlocked.

It was!

No noise. No noise. No noise.

He pulled open the sliding door and was happy to hear only the slightest of grinding sounds. Like a ghost, he slipped into the car and closed the door. The first thing he realized was that the windows were covered with heavy blankets. Only a soft light shone through the layers. In the low illumination, Jack saw that the car's seats were missing, and it was packed with metal cases, instead of places for people to sit.

Jack set his sword down atop one of the cases but kept his pistol handy. Then, he quietly lifted a lid and inspected the bin's wares. There were five framed paintings inside. Each one of them was packed accordingly and separated from its neighbor. They were all the same size, roughly three-feet-squared. It made sense that they were stored in this manner. The lack of light would preserve them.

Also, the Fuhrer was a nut for the stuff.

Most didn't know this, but Hitler had been a very accomplished artist, and was responsible for hundreds of works of art over the years. He had sold them for a living before getting into politics and continued to paint while he was in office. His artwork was incredibly valuable. Jack had even seen a few of his paintings before and was surprised at how good they were.

Curious, Jack carefully lifted the first painting out of the container and looked it over. It depicted a serene mountain landscape, something that would make Bob Ross proud. Snowy hills dotted the horizon with a quaint log cabin situated at the center of it all. It was masterful, yet straightforward. Jack angled the creation so he could read the artist's name.

"Adolf Hitler," he whispered.

He gazed at the framed work with fresh eyes, then looked around the car. He slid the painting back into place and opened the case behind him. It was, likewise, full of artwork. This time, Jack didn't pay attention to the art itself. Instead, he went straight for the signature and found that Hitler had also created it. The next bin contained more of the same thing.

The entire car was, sort of, like Hitler's private art gallery, and to someone like Jack, a man who appreciated World War II history more than most, it was a priceless discovery. He'd never forget this moment in time.

But he still had a job to do.

Emma's muffled shouts turned his attention away from the artwork. There was still something that Jack didn't understand. He pictured Emma's face—her piercing eyes. Then, he visualized the train, a vehicle that had not been operated in decades, pulling away.

There's no way.

Jack turned and looked at the door.

"How are you getting this stuff out of here?"

"Find him!" Emma shouted, seething with rage.

It drove her mad that the only person that stood in her way had somehow survived what should've been a fatal fall into an icy river. It *must've* been Jack that lit the fires. There could've been no one else.

"We've searched everywhere!" Karl called back, helping Jurgen walk. "We can't find him!"

Gunter stepped up close, voice soft. "We've searched this place top to bottom, and still, we've found nothing." He tipped his chin toward the entry tunnel leading back to Auschwitz. "Maybe he ran?"

Emma shook her head, calming some. "No, not this one. He's different." She took a deep breath. "Get the rest of the men down here. We need to get started immediately." Gunter nodded and headed off but was stopped. "Also, tell Piotr to lock down the access point and rejoin the hostages. Tell him that we'll contact him once we've discovered the mountain passage."

"We're still paying him?" Gunter asked, looking unhappy.

Emma nodded. "If we're to make this work, we need him to remain on our side while we're down here," she placed her right hand on his shoulder, "even if it means that he'll have to wait a little bit longer than originally agreed upon.

"And if he refuses?"

"Tell him we'll double his offer—six hundred million dollars." Emma continued before he could argue. "Remember, brother. This isn't a short-term venture." She smiled. "This is it. After this, we'll have everything we've ever dreamed of."

"So," he said, "the bunker?"

"Yes, the bunker. It will be our home for as long as this takes."

Gunter wasn't comfortable with the idea of living underground for months on end, but they had all agreed that it was the only way for their plan to come to fruition.

Emma watched as her brother hurried over to Karl and Jurgen. He took the injured man's arm, quickly speaking to Karl as he did. The other man nodded and hurried off the platform and back down the tunnel, disappearing within seconds.

Until the rest of Emma's team arrived, it would be just her,

Gunter, and Jurgen. They'd need to be on high alert too. Jack Reilly was proving to be a capable adversary—as well as an annoyance.

12

Jack was shocked at how they were going about this. He figured that they'd, at the very least, try and get the antiquated train moving. Jack didn't know whether or not the near-century-old engine could even pull the weight, and it looked as if Emma wasn't going to waste the time and take the chance either way.

They're moving in.

It was a ballsy move for sure. Emma's plan was never to rush in, grab a handful of cash, and then bolt. She was set to play the long, long game. They were going to live in the bunker directly beneath Auschwitz, just as the Nazis had planned to do all those years ago. They could take their time and scout ahead for an exit to the surface. And when they did, they'd finish their plan and sell off both treasures to the highest bidders.

It also meant that Jack wasn't leaving anytime soon.

"Just wonderful," he said, leaning against the wall of the train car. "Guess I'll have to cancel my appointment with my barber."

The more Jack thought about it, not moving any of the treasure was a brilliant thing to do. Transporting it, just hours after a team of gunmen took over a place as widely known as Auschwitz, would've been the wrong move. There'd be too much attention on the camp as it were. Add in the mystery of the vanishing mercenaries, and *BOOM*, you'd—

"Piotr," Jack said, realizing what was going to happen.

The older man, who had, apparently, reacquired his key, was going to cover for Emma for as long as it took. He'd been the museum's trusted director for nearly four decades. No one would suspect that it was him—that he was the inside man. It was his word against no one. All he'd have to do was reseal the office wall beneath the Death Block and go about his life.

Emma probably has her buyers on standby, Jack thought.

Once she emerged with even a pocketful of the treasure, they'd immediately start selling it off piece by piece. The mountains were a perfect location too. At nearly 125 miles away, Emma's people would be able to move freely between here and there without anyone noticing a thing. Then, when the fortune was gone, they could quickly abandon the vault and slip away with their engorged bank accounts bursting at the seams. Jack was witnessing a unique, and incredibly ballsy, heist. Stealing and selling a treasure that no one knew existed.

But Jack knew.

And he was about to be severely outgunned. If he made his move now, it was only Emma, Gunter, and a still recovering Jurgen that he would have to deal with. He had to catch up with Karl regardless—preferably *before* he reached his comrades aboveground. This was the only time Jack would have to reach the surface. He needed to warn someone. If the rest of Emma's team made it down before he could call for help, it would be all but over. Locking the only way out was a problem.

So, as soon as Jack decided to abandon the treasure for a more pressing matter, he flipped the switch and made his move. Silently, he reacquired his sword and backtracked out of the train car and onto the empty half of the platform. He could still hear Emma and Gunter speaking, along with a third person. If Jack had to guess, Jurgen was retelling what had happened back at the book pile.

Jack climbed down onto the tracks and stayed low until he was out of sight and further down the tunnel. He turned his attention to the only thing standing in his way—Karl. Jack kept his flashlight off and crept forward in the dark. The tracks beneath his feet guided him forward, but it was slow-moving. He needed to stay quiet, or all Karl would have to do was spray a volley of bullets back at him. He'd more than likely miss Jack, but there was a one hundred percent chance that the gunshots would alert Emma and the others.

Absolutely no gunfire, Jack decided.

He slid his pilfered Glock into the back of his pants and gripped his Persian scimitar in both hands. He felt like an ancient warrior from out of time. Blade versus bullets. It was a battle he'd assuredly lose if he were noticed. He was literally bringing a knife to a gunfight.

Well, technically, it's a sword, he thought, squinting.

Jack nearly stepped off the railroad tie and twisted his knee. His mind wandered too far toward the conflict ahead and off his current dilemma. He couldn't see shit. Jack was also beyond exhausted, and his body ached all over. Karl, the man who had coldcocked him, was somewhere just up ahead, and, this time, Karl was going to feel more than only Jack's forehead in the bridge of his nose.

He gripped the hilt of his sword harder and zeroed in on the sound of fumbling feet and crumbling stone. Jack stopped and ducked as a beam of light suddenly swept across the tunnel. All he could do was get down on one knee and dip his head as low as possible. Hopefully, his dark hair and jacket concealed him.

Jack waited to be shot, and when it didn't happen, he peeked up and saw that the light wasn't focused and controlled. It was wildly flopping around the tunnel. It was still a ways off too, and over his head. Within the chaotical moving aura was a figure climbing atop a mountainous pile of rubble.

"Karl," Jack whispered, standing.

This was his chance.

Jack rushed forward just as his quarry disappeared through a hole near the ceiling. Now on the other side, Karl wouldn't be able to hear or see Jack's approach. Jack would gain some serious ground. But if he were to use the scimitar, as he had planned, he'd need to be within an arm's reach of Karl.

The passage through the blockage also confirmed Jack's hypothesis from earlier. Emma's team had, indeed, forced their way through the cave-in with a controlled blast. One of the men on her squad wasn't just a gun for hire. One of them was well-versed in the art of blowing crap up.

Probably ex-military, Jack thought.

He'd met a slew of "soldiers of fortune" over the years. Most had been washouts. Some couldn't handle civilian life, or they had too spotty of a record to get a job in any type of law enforcement. So, they went the "private security" route and did jobs under the table in places like the Middle East.

He had thought about pursuing the same career once, but ultimately, he decided to move back home when his grandmother finally started to slow down. She didn't mind living alone, but it had become all-to-clear that she wouldn't be able to do so for much longer—and no way was Jack going to allow her to move into a nursing home. Though, eventually, she did. Her extensive care, and Jack's new career, made it impossible for him to go at it alone.

Quickly, yet cautiously, Jack clicked on Jurgen's flashlight and scaled the mass of stone. He targeted the largest, most-secure boulders he could, skipping entire sections altogether. Unlike Jack's stealthier path, Karl's noisier trail took him from Point A to Point B in a quick, straight line. Jack's path forced him left and right and then left again. It was much slower, but it was infinitely quieter.

Finally, he made it. When he did, he covered the lens of his Mini Maglite with his hand and waited. Karl could still be seen, or rather, his light was still visible. He had continued forward, stopping near where they had left the handcarts.

After another thirty seconds of inaction, Jack extinguished his light and continued down the other side. The descent was awkward and clumsy. He did it all while keeping his eyes on Karl's beam. It had yet to turn back to him.

Jack stepped off the lowest boulder and clipped a smaller stone with his toe. It clattered to the ground and made Jack nearly piss himself. Luckily, Karl's light was still facing forward. Actually, it didn't move at all.

"Dammit," he whispered, crouching, and watching.

Still, even with the noise, the beam of Karl's light didn't waver. He was still next to the second handcart. Confused, and a bit unnerved, Jack slowly crept forward. He stopped in front of the first cart and listened. Nothing. The tunnel was silent. He leaned right and spied the light, noticing something he didn't like.

Karl wasn't holding it.

The mercenary had set it on the second cart's platform. He looked around. *Is he taking a piss?* Swiftly, Jack clicked on his own light and showed it around the tunnel. Karl was nowhere to be seen. It meant that he had known that Jack was incoming. He set a trap.

Jack searched every inch of space around the two handcarts but didn't find a thing. No sign of Karl anywhere. He threw up his hands in frustration and turned around, facing the rear of the second cart.

"Where is this prick?"

A shape slithered out from beneath the cart and launched itself into the air. It took a second for Jack to put two and two together. Karl had, undeniably, set a trap. He had hidden beneath the cart and waited for Jack to lower his defenses.

Unable to get his sword up in time, Jack took Karl's full momentum, including his shoulder, in the sternum. The jolt knocked both Jack's weapon and flashlight away. Each of them clattered off into the darkness. The Mini Maglite landed against the rocky wall and tilted upward. It, combined with Karl's light, gave Jack and his combatant enough to see by.

Before Karl advanced any further, Jack crab-walked backward away from him and stumbled to his feet. Both men were still armed, and Jack was thankful that Karl seemed to be okay with using his bare knuckles and not his gun. Jack didn't want to do anything to change his mind. So, he also lifted his fists instead of going for his pistol.

No guns, Jack reminded himself. He still needed to incapacitate Karl without any bullets being fired. Emma and the others were still in range of the report.

Jack stretched his neck side to side, never once taking his eyes off Karl. The thicker man grinned.

"What's so funny?" Jack asked.

"Having a rough day?" Karl poked.

Jack stepped forward and pointed at Karl's nose. "How's the face?"

Karl's smile turned into a scowl, and he bull-rushed his opponent.

Jack met him halfway, stalemating the German for a moment. Regrettably, Jack's fatigue gave in, and Karl drove him backward. He was about to go down and decided, that if he did, he'd bring Karl with him.

But his opponent righted himself.

No!

Jack gripped the man's shirt, and he leapt into the air. With his chest in the bigger man's face, Jack bearhugged Karl's head and wrapped his legs around his waist. He speedily locked his ankles around the small of Karl's back and rode him like a bucking bronco.

The mercenary's muffled shouts of anger turned into moans of pain as Jack started rotating elbow strikes into Karl's exposed temples. Everything about his unconventional method of attack worked up until Karl drove Jack's back into the rocky wall. Jack hit hard, but he didn't let go. He got in another pair of elbow strikes just above Karl's left eye before he was dislodged and tossed aside.

The thicker man stumbled away and tripped on one of the elevated railroad tracks. Jack scrambled to his feet, ducked his head, and drove himself into Karl's midsection. The already off-balance oaf was forced backward, right into the rear platform of the second handcart. The jarring blow knocked the flashlight from its perch.

Just in the nick of time too.

As Jack stepped back to catch his breath, Karl drew his pistol and pulled the trigger. Jack evaded the bullet, and before Karl got off a second shot, they were cast into near darkness when the bulb shattered. Now, the only thing left was Jack's small Maglite, but it was too far away and too low of a lumen count to be much help.

Jack took two more steps to his left and then dove for where he last saw Karl. Hands out in front of him, he clawed for the weapon but found only his adversary's face in its place.

That'll do.

Now, instead of trying to disarm his foe, Jack attempted to blind him. He dug his filthy fingers into Karl's eyes and was happy to hear the man howl in protest. In the dim light, Jack saw Karl's gun hand swing toward him. Keeping his left hand engaged, he swatted the weapon away with the back of his balled right fist. Jack grabbed the back of Karl's head and pulled him toward him by his hair—like the German was his lover.

He didn't kiss him, though.

He did quite the opposite.

Jack, once more, smashed his forehead into the man's face. The blow staggered Karl, but it didn't knock him out. Dizzy in his own right, Jack shook his head and backed away from the bleeding, wailing mercenary.

Karl fell to his hands and knees and grabbed for his discarded pistol. Jack halted his attempt by kicking him as hard as he could, right in the head. His boot caught Karl just above his left ear, and he instantly crumpled in on himself. Hands on his hips, Jack stood slightly bent over at the waist and took a handful of deep breaths. He felt ten times worse than he had just minutes earlier.

Jack wiped the blood from his lip and laughed. "Boy, am I gonna be sore in the morning."

13

Some might say that stripping your unconscious enemy naked and zip-tying his or her arms and legs together was childish. Well, if that was true, then Jack Reilly was nothing more than an oversized pre-teen. Initially, he searched Karl for anything useful. Then, Jack got the splendid idea to shame him.

"I'm not gonna kill you," Jack said, tying him up, "but I'm sure as hell going to humiliate you." He laughed. "Should make an interesting mugshot."

Jack could have, just as quickly, ended the man's life, but that wasn't his way. He wasn't a heartless murderer. Yes, he had killed his share of people in the past. Back then, he had killed for his country, not himself. All of his targets were terrible individuals as well.

"Kind of like you," he said, flicking Karl's forehead.

The first thing Jack did was take the guy's weapons and ammo—all of it. Next to go was his Kevlar vest. Karl's backpack was full of survivalist supplies like food and water, but there were also two sticks of plastic explosives and a timer detonator. His tactical mask was present too.

It looks like I found Emma's demolitions expert, Jack thought, gazing back up toward the hole in the rubble.

The style of detonator that had been used made sense since they were underground. In a typical setting, you'd use one that generated a radio signal. In this case, with tons and tons of stone around them, a timer was better suited.

And as far as Karl was concerned...

Jack rolled him onto his stomach and tied his wrists to the rear left wheel of the handcart. Then, he tied Karl's ankles to the other rear wheel. No one would find him unless they looked hard enough, or until the man woke up and cried for help. Jack fixed that issue and stuffed one of the mercenary's rank socks into his mouth.

Armed to the teeth with a bigger knife, an HK416 battle rifle, and a second Glock 19 pistol, Jack was ready for anything. He turned and faced the pile of rocks but didn't advance. Karl wasn't supposed to return right away. Gunter ordered him topside to talk things over with Piotr and to retrieve the rest of their men.

It gave Jack an idea, though, he'd have to go against his beliefs and willingly get his hands dirty—*really* dirty. He'd more than likely have to kill someone. Probably even a few someones.

Earlier, Emma had shown off the six gunmen positioned atop the ring of the kitchen buildings. Their job was to watch over the hostages and nothing else. They were also ordered to shoot them on sight if any of them made a run for it, or if Jack disobeyed Emma. Jack's plan was doable if that were the case. None of the rooftop gunmen would be expecting an attack from behind.

Karl's combat knife was sheathed on Jack's chest for easy access, along with a handsfree, tactical right-angle flashlight. The man's sidearm was situated inside Jack's new thigh holster. Karl's carbine was slung across his back, and his ammo supply was plentiful. Jurgen's pistol was tucked into the back of his pants to be used as a last-ditch option. The last time Jack was dressed like this—for combat—had been during the incident in Mosul.

He thought he'd sworn off war forever.

"Well," Jack drew Karl's Glock and checked it over, "so much for that."

Jack flicked on his chest-mounted light. He spun and stomped back toward Auschwitz, leaving his scimitar behind. It was time to be a modern-day warrior, not an archaic one.

The best part about his idea was that no one in Emma's topside team would know what hit them. He owned the element of surprise. None of her people could know that he had successfully escaped capture and was coming back to free the hostages.

To put it plainly, Jack's plan was bat-shit crazy.

But it was *his* kind of crazy.

"And what's that got to do with guano?"

With no threat in sight, Jack kept his weapons holstered, and he set out at a brisk powerwalk. It was as brisk of a pace as he could muster. His body was tightening up fast. Soon, he'd be forced to voluntarily take a dip in the temple's ice-cold pool to numb his muscles and joints.

He thought about moving Karl and trying to operate the handcart solo but recalled how hard it was for him to get it going, even with the help of Emma *and* Gunter. There was no way he could do it by himself. Plus, if someone came searching for him and Karl and found the cart missing, Jack's plan would be ruined. The only place he could've gone was back toward the camp.

Leaving it behind was his best option.

Jack could just see the lit train station up ahead. He felt like a moth to a flame and broke into a jog. He burst into the illuminated station with joy in his heart. Just being back near civilization was a godsend. It meant that he was *this much* closer to normalcy.

He struggled to pull himself up onto the empty platform, making it after two attempts.

Jack adjusted the straps of his vest and wiped the sweat off his forehead. "Damn, I forgot how heavy this crap is!"

He took a second to catch his breath before making his way to the stairs. As he climbed them, he remembered to skirt around the worn wet spot from before. He shouldered his rifle and peeked inside the bunker. The room within was empty. Satisfied that no one had been sent to check on Emma's team, he stepped inside and clicked on the weapon's barrel-mounted light. Not needing them both, Jack turned off the right-angle light attached to his vest.

The lights within the bunker didn't respond well to the switch being thrown. Only a few of them were on, leaving much of the underground living space in darkness. It felt like a scene out of *The Last of Us*. It was one of Jack's favorite video game series, just behind Naughty Dog's other bestselling franchise, *Uncharted*.

He panned left, then right, never once locking in on one spot. The power of the LED bulb mounted onto his carbine's barrel was ridiculously powerful—more powerful than anything he'd ever used before. He could see everything in each room with no trouble. The doorway directly in front of him held the makeshift movie theater. After that was the gym. If there were someone down here with him, he'd know it.

And so would they.

Thinking better of it, Jack stepped into the theater and flicked off his light, deciding to go at it with the limited lighting provided by his chest-mounted lamp as well as the handful of lights that were lit inside the bunker. He was happy he had made the decision when he did, because just as Jack extinguished his rifle's beam, and before he reignited his chest-mounted variant, he heard feet banging down the metal stairs. Quickly, he pressed himself up against the wall of the theater. He inched sideways until only his head was poking out. From there, he saw straight through the gym and to the lit access point.

Another of Emma's men appeared and called out.

"Gunter?" he shouted. "Hey, Gunter?"

Jack watched the man flip on a barrel-mounted light similar to his. The mercenary stepped off the stairs and went right, toward the weapons locker. Jack silently moved forward into the gym. Now, he was in striking distance with any of his various armaments. This guy needed to be taken down quietly, and since Jack had no sound suppressor, he went with the only option he possessed.

He slowly unsheathed Karl's heavy-duty tactical knife.

Add it to the list with pistols and carbines because Jack was also elite with a blade. Staying low, he crept up behind the newcomer as he entered the weapons cache. Just when Jack was about to make his move, his boot found a small piece of debris and made a crunching sound that rivaled a cannon blast. The stillness of the environment made the noise infinitely louder than it truly was.

With nowhere to go, Jack crouched beneath the gunman's flashlight beam. Miraculously, it passed harmlessly over his head, and he wasn't seen. The mercenary was too focused on the bunker to notice a man squatting within a few feet from him. Jack was also currently out of his line of sight. A raised rifle created a blind spot directly under it—right where Jack was now.

Jack was so close—close enough to jab the guy in the gut with his knife. He didn't, though. Instead, Jack patiently waited for him to turn around and step away. Even if his blade did find flesh, the gunman still would've had the capability to speak. Jack planned on taking that ability away with nothing more than the flick of his wrist.

Another overhead light suddenly blinked to life behind him, bathing him in its ambiance. As a result, his shadow was cast on the wall across the room—right where his target could see it. Before the gunman could react, Jack leapt on his back, forgoing the use of his knife. He'd silence the man with his bare hands instead.

The stunned German was too slow to get his arms up to block the attack, and Jack successfully wrapped the crook of his left elbow around his neck. Locked in, Jack drove his right foot into the back of his adversary's knee. The combined attacks caused the man to go down.

In one motion, Jack rolled to the side and wrapped his legs around the mercenary's waist, securing his ankles together—much like he did in his brawl with Karl. Only, this time, Jack was using a maneuver called a "rear naked choke." The idea was to cut off your opponent's airway and render him unconscious. Based on his wrestling partner's movements, Jack was doing a fabulous job.

"Shhh, shhh, shhh," Jack cooed, yanking back hard. "It's okay. Time...for a nice...relaxing...nap."

As the seconds passed, his enemy's responses dwindled down to nothing. Ten more seconds and Jack let go. He shoved him aside and got to his feet. The last time he'd done that had been the year he started in Yellowstone. It was a long story, but it began with someone badmouthing Bull's people. The "conflict" ended with the potbelly asshole landing flat on his back, in the mud, and somewhere off in dreamland.

Kneeling, Jack collected his knife and sheathed it. He checked the mercenary's pulse next. But Gunter's buddy wasn't breathing. Even if Jack wanted to perform CPR, he couldn't. Another set of feet could be heard pounding down the circular steps behind and above him. Either Jack needed to take the next one head-on, or he needed to conceal the dead man's body before he was discovered.

Or...

Jack got an idea.

He slid beneath the lowest section of steps, leaving Humpty to be found by Dumpty. Once again, he slid his blade free and readied it. The second guy's reaction was instantaneous. He rushed toward his fallen comrade and called out. "Jonas!" Either his voice was naturally high, or he was unbelievably young. Jack forced the incoming memory of the boy from Mosul from his mind, and instead, he floated after Jonas' colleague.

When the second man leaned over the body, Jack pounced.

Faster than a cobra strike, Jack covered this one's mouth with his free hand and swiftly yanked his knife hand from left to right. Then, Jack stepped back and kicked the bleeding mercenary in the small of his back. The mortal injury, combined with his off-balance stance, sent the German sprawling to the ground.

Jack didn't stick around to watch him die. He turned for the stairs and started the next phase of his rescue operation. He had just killed two men in less than a minute in a place that had already seen its fair share of death.

"The Devil's pet guards the way."

Emma looked up from the Himmler journal and thought about what she had just read. It sounded like some sort of creature had taken up residence in the tunnels. She wasn't sure where, but Himmler wouldn't have written it unless it was true.

"That was eighty years ago."

Nothing was for sure now. There was a chance that whatever his *pet* had been didn't exist anymore. But if it did, what could it be?

Emma closed the journal and slipped it back into her vest. She stood and tried to wipe the building tiredness from her face but was unsuccessful. Then, it hit her. She knew of an animal that fit the description, and something dangerous enough for Himmler to have added it to his book. Looking around her feet, Emma was happy to see nothing.

She sighed, feeling foolish. If they hadn't seen any of them yet, they were probably no longer in the area. The winter weather would've driven them deep underground.

As the Bible says, Satan once offered Adam and Eve an apple. The form he took has long been used as the representation of evil—the symbol of "the Devil's pet" from Himmler's journal.

14

Jack was nearly at the top, and he was winded and cold. His mind and body had been through a lot, even more than an average mission back with his Delta team. Most of those operations had been more mentally stressful than anything else.

The air rushing in was crisp, and his clothes were still damp. The warmth of the fire down in the Templar stronghold beckoned him to turn around. So did the treasure, for that matter. He stopped and readied himself, shouldering his rifle. As much as his body was telling him to stop, he still had a job to do. As it was, this was his first solo assignment. His Delta team had been precisely that—a team.

At this moment, Jack Reilly was an expertly trained, one-man battery. He strapped on Karl's tactical mask and tested it out. His breathing was okay, and it fit snug enough that it wouldn't shift and annoy him too much. Concealing his identity was paramount. He was an armed American—with no ID—inside a World War II-era concentration camp turned state museum.

"Okay," he told himself, his voice slightly muffled, "let's do this."

Jack rushed up the remaining stairs and nearly bulldozed into Piotr. The museum director didn't get off easy, though. Jack delivered a bone-jarring uppercut to the older man's chin with the stock of his carbine. The blow sent the Nazi sympathizer sprawling to the ground without a response.

One of Emma's men came rushing into the office from the hallway and was met with a three-round burst to the exposed part of his upper chest. Two of the bullets found flesh, flinging the man back through the doorway along with a splatter of blood.

Jack stood still, locked in, breathing hard. He couldn't believe what he'd just done, and how quickly he'd done it. He was embattled, but he knew he was here for a reason. With his abilities, he was going to save everyone that was at risk.

Blinking out of the shock he was in, he looked down at the

cowering traitor. He bent over Piotr and ripped the key from his neck. "I'll take this." He pocketed it and stepped away, but stopped and looked back over his shoulder. "I'll be back for you later." Piotr clawed at Jack's legs but was too weak to impede him.

Jack turned his attention back to the mission, and he smoothly made his way to the doorway. He refused to look at the man he had just shot. Jack listened and waited for footsteps. Sooner or later, someone would come to check on Piotr and the guard.

Jack's eyes floated around his surroundings. The Cellar walls would reduce the rifle's report, possibly concealing it altogether. With a little luck on his side, he was able to slip out of the office and check the main hallway unperturbed. The way was empty.

Weapon forward, Jack quickly stepped heel-to-toe and made his way to the stairs. Again, he waited for any sign that his counterassault had been noticed. No one came down to check, so he headed up the stairs, taking a headcount as he did.

Not counting Karl, he'd taken out three of Emma's people since leaving the treasure room. She had happily boasted about the six gunmen atop of the kitchen rooftops, though it was while he'd been fighting off a brutal headache. In reality, he hadn't seen much. There were also other men roaming the grounds, from what she had said. The trio he'd come across here was proof enough.

But how many more were there?

Jack took the steep stairs two at a time, intent on finding out. He hit the landing and snapped his carbine up. Nothing greeted him, and he continued up to the first floor. The dense concrete and brick walls of the Death Block had successfully acted as the world's largest sound suppressor.

"Ernst?"

Jack stumbled when he heard the voice. He had been about to turn into the central corridor. Luckily, he stopped before he was spotted. The newcomer must've been the one stationed outside the front door. Jack vaguely recalled Gunter ordering someone to stay put there.

"Ernst?" the man called out again.

Jack pressed himself up against the wall just outside the stairs to the Cellar. He needed the guy to come to him, but to do so without being suspicious.

"*Ja?*" Jack asked. It was one of the only German words he knew. The other one word he knew was from *Die Hard*. Hans Gruber's men shouted it a lot. It translated to, "Quickly!" So, Jack decided to use that one too.

"*Schnell!*" he shouted.

"*Schnell?*" the man asked back, confused.

"*Ja,*" Jack replied.

Ernst's friend broke out into Jack in a string of garbled gibberish. Unsure of how to respond, Jack stayed silent. The guard stepped into the building, with a clunk of his boot, and repeated what he had just said. As he did before, Jack kept his mouth shut.

"Ernst?"

"*Ja?*" Jack repeated.

Jack's man was baffled, so much so that he started coming his way to figure out what the hell was going on. Without a sound, Jack leaned his carbine against the wall and drew his newly acquired tactical knife. He needed to time his next series of moves correctly.

A shadow appeared from around the corner.

"Ernst?"

Nope, sorry. Not Ernst.

Just before he saw the German, Jack leapt out of his cover, slapped the man's drawn pistol from his hand. He swiftly plunged the tip of his blade into the base of the trooper's throat, just below his Adam's apple. Jack kicked the weapon away and sidestepped the gagging man, leaving the knife buried in place. He kicked out the back of the mercenary's knees and he picked up his rifle. Then, he turned and headed for the door.

Before he stepped outside, Jack glanced over his shoulder. The guy was floundering in his own blood.

"Sorry, buddy," Jack said, dejected, "but you dug your own grave by signing up with this lot."

Shouldering his carbine, he took one long breath and calmed his pole-vaulting nerves. The sun was still out, but it was significantly lower than it had been when he had first entered the Death Block. He'd been underground for a few hours, at least. He confirmed as much when he checked his watch. When he did, he also paused to look at his bracelet. The one on his left wrist stood for "strength."

He would need the strength of Samson to finish what he had set out to accomplish. Jack hated every minute of what he was doing. But his mind went to the pair of kids that had helped him to his feet inside the kitchen's central loading area. If he decided to quit and walk away, their lives would be in peril. Plus, he was too far into his counterstrike to just stop. Someone was bound to find the men he had just killed, and when they did, the hostages were toast.

"Come on, Jack." He lifted the weapon higher. "Get your ass moving."

Looking down the sights of his carbine, Jack quickly descended the steps of the Death Block. Out in the open, he made himself a smaller target and knelt, focusing on the alleyway to his left. There was a dead-end to his right—the Black Wall.

Seeing nothing, Jack stood and was buffeted by a crisp breeze. It stung his eyes, making them water. Blinking the liquid away, he pushed aside the dropping temperature on his damp skin and moved on. He was currently at the grounds between the Death Block and Block 10, the medical experimentation ward, which had been headed up by the infamous Josef Mengele.

Mengele was known as the Fuhrer's "Angel of Death," and may have been a worse human being than Himmler, or even Hitler himself. Most historians agreed that the things Mengele had done here were some of the worst war crimes ever recorded. But the worst thing of all was that Mengele had lived into his sixties down in South America. At least Hitler and Himmler had died when they did.

As Jack did before, he stopped and covertly peeked out into the crisscrossing "street." From here, the enclosed loading area containing the hostages was around to his right. Next, he needed to make a left at the second intersection. Then, all he'd have to do was continue straight until bullets flew. But that wasn't the way he'd go now. If he wanted to battle the rooftop mercenaries head-on, and speedily die, it was the perfect plan.

Jack went straight and hopped the curb. The earth between the pair of inmate infirmaries dipped toward the middle. The channel was designed to help with runoff during heavy downpours. The lawn, including the grass in the drainage ditch, was neatly manicured and covered in a light layer of snow. At the moment, the dusting had stopped. Jack hoped it stayed that way.

He was wet and freezing.

"Stop bitching, Jack," he muttered, jaw clenched. "Better to be cold than Ernst."

The next crossroad was up ahead, and he nearly charged over it without first pausing to see if the coast was clear. He wasn't as attentive as he should've been. There were too many unknowns, and as hard as he tried to ignore it, he was cold. His hands trembled. Still, Jack didn't care whether he was out of practice or not. He should've been able to control himself better.

"You're better than this."

Stopping in between two identical infirmaries, Jack knelt in the chilled, snow-covered grass, backseating the rising anger he felt towards it. He took in the scene and spotted one of Emma's men off to his right. The guy was still three buildings away, and his back was to Jack position. He wanted nothing more than to shoot the mercenary, here and now, but he needed to proceed with caution. Jack couldn't see if this one had a friend nearby.

Plus, the concussive report of his rifle would give him away. He wasn't down in the Cellar anymore. Everything he did from here on out needed to be accomplished quietly. That would be easier said than done, considering there was nowhere to hide while on the main paths. Jack needed to traverse the distance between himself and the gunman, three buildings worth, about two hundred feet, and pray the guy didn't turn around.

"Here we go," he said, stepping out.

He walked, slightly hunched, keeping his sights trained on the mercenary's back as he glided along. Special Forces soldiers were taught to step lightly and to do so quickly.

After each brick building, he stepped off the road and rechecked his surroundings. His target had yet to move an inch, which was good, but it also unnerved Jack. It meant that his target could move at any time.

Or, he's some weird gun-toting scarecrow.

As he approached the last building, Jack groped his chest for Karl's knife. It wasn't there. He had left it in the throat of one of Emma's men. Not the smartest decision, as it were.

Jack figured that all the guys would be outfitted similarly since their endgame was all one and the same. Everyone involved with Emma was supposed to join her and her exploratory team below the Death Block once the treasure had been located. Not only would their packs be stocked similarly, but Jack guessed their weapons would be mostly identical. So far, everyone except for Emma carried an HK416. It made sense that they'd also have a knife sheathed on their chests as Karl had.

Let's hope.

Jack looped his carbine over his shoulder, but stopped and grinned. He didn't need the gunman's blade. He had another one. From around his back, Jack pulled free the smaller, German trench knife that he'd pilfered from the underground weapons cache. At this point, the blade was his most trusted ally. It wasn't exactly Karl's tactical variation, but it'd do the job just fine.

Knife at the ready, Jack crept up behind his target, and froze when the guard casually turned around and leveled his rifle at Jack's gut.

Had Jack been found out? No, the mercenary was just as surprised as Jack was. Before he could pull the trigger, Jack pushed the barrel aside and launched his attack, jabbing the blade tip at the gunman's neck. Impressively, the German didn't try and shoot Jack.

He blocked the strike with the frame of his weapon. Both men struggled against the other. Just as Jack ripped the carbine from his opponent's grasp, he lost his knife in the same manner.

The guard opened his mouth to call for help but didn't get the chance to do so. Jack thrust his right palm into the trooper's chin. The blow caused him to bite his tongue.

Never one to shy away from fighting dirty, Jack kicked the mercenary in the groin as hard as he could. The shot pitched him forward and Jack added a quick rising elbow strike to his face. As the gunman tilted backward, he grabbed Jack's vest and pulled him along. He balled his fist and tried to punch Jack but was surprised when Jack grabbed him and pulled him in close.

As he'd done multiple times with Karl, Jack used his own head as a device of pain. He slammed his forehead into the bridge of the shooter's nose, crushing it. But this time, Jack also felt the effect.

He shook his head and blinked his eyes. *I gotta stop doing that.*

Jack didn't get as clean of an impact as he'd done with Karl. He saw spots his time. The other guy fared worse, though.

Nearly out on his feet, Jack kicked him in the left knee twice, weakening his base. Then, he grasped both of the assassin's shoulder straps and yanked him around to the left. Building up some momentum, Jack stopped three-quarters of the way around, stuck out his foot and tripped his adversary.

He sent the black-clad man face first into the side of the brick infirmary. He slumped to the ground but didn't stay down. *No, you don't!* Jack stomped on the back of the German's head. The impact drove his skull back into the building and he went down for good.

Breathing hard, Jack checked to see if anyone had witnessed their tussle. He breathed easier when he found the area clear. Jack quickly collected both of their belongings and dragged the unconscious killer around the side of the building, dumping him behind some nearby shrubs.

Before he started up his mission again, he dug into the guy's pack and found another two sticks of plastic explosives and two bottles of water. Dazed from a lack of real rest, and the latest, and hopefully last, headbutt, Jack procured a bottle, opened the cap, and splashed some of it on his face. The liquid rapidly reacted to the outside temperature and its sting instantaneously jolted Jack out of his delirium. He gulped down the rest of it and stood.

Leaning against the infirmary, Jack huffed and puffed.

"No!"

A voice cried out from somewhere up ahead. It was all Jack needed to pick up his gear and get moving. There were still more of Emma's men out there, and he needed to remove their presence from the camp.

15

This time around, Jack could inspect the grounds surrounding the kitchen square from afar. The last time he was here, he'd been laying on his side, fighting off a splitting headache. From what he could tell, there was only one way in and out. A simple double-door wooden gate was all that was in his way from freeing the hostages.

As well as the rooftop gunmen, he thought, leaning out from behind the building across from the kitchen.

Jack took a few minutes to watch the guards. Two were stationed at the northern end of the horizontal rectangle. Two more were at the southern end. There was also one man posted on each side—six in total. Emma's warning about them was factual and not just an intimidation tactic.

There wasn't a direct route up to the roof from what Jack could see. He was going to have to do a little more recon first. He waited for the two guards closest to him to turn. It didn't happen right away. When one moved off, the other one didn't, and vice versa. Five minutes of waiting went by before Jack finally got his chance. Luckily, the dipping temperature was making the men increasingly uncomfortable and it was becoming more and more difficult to stand still. And Jack agreed. For just a moment, both men turned their backs to the front of the entrance—to where he was.

Stepping lightly, Jack sprinted across the street. He reflexively ducked under the bar of the gallows even though it was much too high to hit. He flattened himself against the front façade. The roof hung over the base of the building enough to conceal his presence from anyone above him. With nothing to use as a ladder, Jack sidestepped to his right and headed toward the southwest corner of the kitchens.

He quickly checked that the coast was clear and slunk around the corner, continuing along the western face. Up ahead, there was a stout offshoot structure built into the northwest corner of the kitchens. It stood seven feet high and had a garbage can situated next to it.

Bingo!

Jack hurried forward and slid atop the four-way concrete waste bin. Its thick plastic cover creaked and gave beneath his weight but held enough for him to get to his knees. He immediately spotted two guards. One of them was at his two o'clock and another at his ten o'clock. Luckily, the setting sun was at his back. If they looked his way, the low rays would conceal him to a degree. Still, he needed to move fast.

The entirety of the long northern section of roofing was dotted with smokestacks, twelve in all. Jack quickly scrambled up and shinnied behind the first of them. They were just thick enough to conceal him.

Now came the hard part. Jack knew that as soon as he opened fire, all six of the shooters would turn their attention, and their weapons, on him.

I need to better the odds.

From his coverage, he should be able to take out three—maybe four—of the six gunmen with relative ease. They were sitting ducks, entirely out in the open. The biggest problem he'd have was with the two on his side of the kitchen. There was ample cover between him and them. Still, two against one, in any situation, was better than six versus one.

Now!

Jack spun to his left and shouldered his HK416. The world around him slowed down. With steady aim, he aimed high and gently squeezed the trigger of his rifle twice. Both rounds bypassed the top of the shooter's Kevlar vest and entered his body through the base of his larynx.

Jack shifted his aim left, and he pumped bullets into shooter number two. One found flesh. Two impacted the off-balance man's vest with the force of a wrecking ball and knocked him down.

Troopers three and four were much farther away. Instead of aiming high, Jack pumped volleys of high caliber projectiles into their unprotected legs. Both gunmen stumbled and fell forward, down into the sea of hostages.

With no time to celebrate, he spun back into cover and waited as the smokestack was pummeled with return fire from the two men on the same rooftop as him. In the chaos of everything, the two mercenaries that fell forward into the pool of hostages had their weapons torn away as soon as they hit. Jack didn't see who relieved the shooters of their arms, but he hoped it was the captured museum security team.

Emma did say there were zero causalities during their takeover.

Jack took a second look and was happy to see that the pair were dressed in identical police-style uniforms. They looked comfortable with the weapons too.

Jack grinned and waved his hand.

They spotted him and waved back.

He swiftly made his move to the subsequent smokestack. Then, the next. Bullets flew as the guards pinned down the two remaining shooters. Jack switched to his Glock, keeping his left hand empty, not that he liked shooting a pistol one-handed. It wasn't as easy as the movies made it out to be. He ducked behind the fifth smokestack after a pair of projectiles whizzed by his right ear.

One of Emma's men stepped out and turned his carbine down at the people below. Jack snapped up his gun and put four rounds into his neck and shoulder area. Seven more impacted the trooper's chest and abdomen, originating from the guards below. The gunman was sent sprawling to the slanted roof. Jack pressed his back against the sixth smokestack, almost done.

He moved off again—and was tackled to the hard rooftop. His Glock was jerked free, and his rifle was pinned beneath him. It happened so fast that he barely had time to dodge the descending knife blade. He tilted his head to the left and thrust his hands to the right. The force of his retaliation made his attacker lean in close. Jack reached up and grabbed him by the vest strap. He lifted both of his feet underneath him, and with all his might, he flipped the knifeman over his head, bouncing him off the nearest smokestack.

Both men were now unarmed, though Jack's adversary looked confident in his hand-to-hand combat skills. But, so was Jack. Fists raised, Jack stepped forward and quickly stopped when the other man drew a pistol from around his back. He leveled it at Jack's chest, but he fired not shot. The mercenary was taken down in a barrage of bullets. Stunned, Jack turned his attention to the guards below. There were four of them now, and each one held a rifle or pistol.

They had saved his life.

Jack gave them a quick salute and collected his gear.

He slid off the roof and was helped to the ground by a group of unarmed bystanders. Each of them repeatedly thanked Jack for rescuing them, but he paid them no real attention. He focused his words on the armed guards who listened intently.

"Call the police and tell them this was organized by Emma and Gunter Schmidt, as well as Piotr Symanski." The last name made Jack cringe. These were the museum director's coworkers, after all.

"Piotr?" one of the guards asked.

Jack nodded. "It's true. He's a Nazi through and through."

All four of Piotr's colleagues looked as if they'd like to have a word with the man. For now, Jack gave them the short version of what had happened and what the group was looking for, leaving out the part that involved them actually finding the treasure. He also left out the discovery of the Knights Templar. Jack couldn't trust anyone with what he knew. Even though the guards had helped him, it didn't mean that they were completely exonerated of any wrongdoing. Even if only one other employee were in on it with Piotr, everything Jack was trying to protect would be at risk.

"You two," he pointed to the men on his left, "come with me. You," he motioned to the pair on his right, "watch after the people here and protect them, just in case there are any more of Piotr's friends around."

Before Jack and his newest best friends could hurry away, he was tackled from behind. Glancing down, he saw a pair of delicate hands wrap around his waist and squeeze. He looked over his shoulder and saw who it was that had embraced him. It was the girl—the girl he had made an important promise to.

Jack turned and smiled beneath his facemask. He felt his cheeks scrape against the material as they rose.

"See," he said, "I told you that you'd be okay."

The young girl smiled back and waved as Jack and the two guards hurried toward the Death Block. He quickly led them inside and then down into the Cellar offices, swiftly bypassing the carnage he had left behind. Jack stepped aside and allowed the duo to apprehend Piotr, who immediately started wailing empty threats at them in English. He began foretelling of a time when the next Fuhrer would rise and demolish everything, rebuilding the world in his image—the Nazi image.

Jack rolled his eyes and stepped away.

"Where are you going?" one of the guards asked.

Jack tipped his head back toward the bunker entrance. "This isn't over yet."

He stepped inside and saw something he had missed earlier. On the floor, just inside the hidden room, was another lock. Jack knelt and inspected it, removing Piotr's key from his pocket. Curious, he slid it inside. It fit perfectly. It gave Jack an idea. If he locked himself inside, no one would be able to follow him. But no one from Emma's exploratory team would be able to leave either, not without blowing the wall to bits and pieces. That was unlikely to happen, though. Jack knew Emma and the others wouldn't chance bringing the Death Block down on top of them.

He looked up at one of the guards. "Make sure no one tries to follow me. It isn't safe."

"What's down there?" he asked.

Jack told him, or rather, he told of a possible truth.

Staring the man hard in the eyes, Jack twisted the key, and said, "Death."

The wall sprang to life and resealed itself. He removed the key from the lock and pocketed it once more. Getting to his feet, he turned and disappeared down the staircase. Jack clambered his way back down into the bunker, his current wind nearly spent.

The first thing he did was ditch the facemask. He gladly ripped it away and tossed it aside. He gave himself a minute to collect himself before continuing straight through the subterranean community to the train station. The steps to the platform passed by in a blur, as did his descent onto the tracks. Jack grumbled out a curse and started off. He used his barrel-mounted light this time. There was no way to know whether anyone had come back to check on Karl.

Knowing my luck, they did.

The best news was that no one could contact the team topside. As far as Emma knew, her people were still in control. Jack needed to diffuse the situation down here. There was no reason for anyone else to die today, including Emma and the others.

Like he'd done with Karl, Jack was perfectly fine with pacifying the remaining mercenary force using nonlethal measures. Unfortunately, the same couldn't be said about the men upstairs, and those in the bunker. There was no way around killing them.

Jack's light landed on the last place he'd seen Karl.

He stopped cold. "Shit." Karl wasn't there.

Fifty feet from the handcart, Jack knelt and scanned the tunnel ahead for movement. There was none. He got to his feet and hauled ass to the cart. The man's bonds had been cut and dumped. Even the remains of his clothes were missing.

"See," Jack said, under his breath, "this is what I get for being nice."

Jack regretted not putting Karl in the ground. His compassion for life was a wartime flaw. It had gotten in the way and bitten him in the ass. He cracked his neck and readjusted the position of his rifle's stock.

"Well, I guess it's time to clean up the mess."

Just inside the narrow side tunnel, Karl sat and waited for Jack to pass. As much as he wanted to, the plan wasn't to kill him. The American would still prove to be a useful deterrent against an incursion from above. So, he'd wait for Jack to get further ahead, and then he'd follow close behind and strike when the time was right.

Gunter had finally come to check on him, finding Karl awake and gagged with a damp sock. Strangely, they found his clothes folded into a neat pile atop the deck of the handcart. Jack had taken the time to strip him nude and then politely set aside his clothing.

"He's a very odd man," Gunter said as Karl dressed.

Gone were Karl's Kevlar vest, backpack, and weapons. Gunter loaned him his pistol and advised him to rejoin the rest of the team back inside the treasure room. Karl swiftly declined the order, much to the chagrin of his commanding officer. His reasoning was sound, however. He said he'd much rather wait for the man who had humiliated him.

Karl growled. "I shall do to him what he failed to do to me."

He was going to kill Jack, but not before torturing him for a while. He wanted to make the bastard squeal. Karl wanted to have a little fun before he exacted his revenge.

16

Jack descended the pile of rubble and then snuck his way up to the treasure room's entrance, extinguishing his rifle's light en route. He searched for his targets but found none. The room seemed to be abandoned.

"Dammit," Jack whispered, digging into his backpack. He didn't like what he *didn't* see.

The scene before him was a nerve-racking one, and not just because the loot had been left unguarded. Jack's presence should've been expected. He anticipated a fight. He quickly looked over his shoulder and waited for movement. An attack from behind was an option. He saw nothing except darkness. So, he turned his attention back to his work on the tunnel wall, tucking his contingency plan deep into a fracture in the rock.

If the enormous room truly was lifeless, then all he'd have to do was come back and deactivate his little friend. But if the room wasn't empty, and Emma was, indeed, waiting for him, then Jack's surprise would be an explosive one to witness.

"It's gonna be a blast," he said, packing up and ducking in behind the rear of the train.

As an alternative to beelining straight to the platform, Jack stayed down below on the tracks. He did stop and eyed the left-hand platform. It was the last place he had seen Emma, Gunter, and Jurgen before getting into his tiff with Karl at the handcart.

But no one was home.

He got low and squeezed between the right-hand wheels and the concrete wall. It was a tight fit, and he had to scuttle forward like a crippled crab. Cramped, but moving steadily, Jack made it to the junction between the third and fourth cars before finally hearing someone's voice.

Emma stepped out from behind a statue of an Egyptian pharaoh. She was followed closely by Gunter and Jurgen. Nothing about the way they were acting was off. They were just calmly speaking to one another while motioning back to the treasure.

"I really need to learn German," Jack said, not understanding a lick of it. So, he concentrated on their body language. They kept pointing back up the slope to where Jack had initially entered the room.

"The temple?"

They'd found the hidden Templar stronghold and were just now returning from their hike. Had Jack read this whole thing wrong? Weren't they wise to him? What about Karl, where was he?

"Hmmm."

Either way, Jack didn't like the smell of it. It was fishy at best. The space between the cars was too tight to use his carbine. So, he turned and slowly hauled himself out from under the train. When he was halfway up, someone reached down and gave him a hand.

The *hand* belonged to Karl—and it was more of a fist to the face than a gesture of aid. It connected like a sledgehammer. Jack did his best Roger Rabbit impression, and he saw stars. Then, the fully clothed mercenary gripped the straps of Jack's vest—his vest—and pulled him up the rest of the way. Jack's face was at a convenient knee-height level, and Karl took the opportunity to pummel him with a series of thunderous strikes. Jack blocked most of them, but two landed solidly and stupefied him further.

Half out of it, Jack was thrown to the ground and rolled onto his back. He was stripped of his gear, but thankfully, not his clothes. Seconds later, he was surrounded. Wincing, he looked up, spotting a blurry Karl first. The German's bruised face and black eyes had darkened immensely since he last saw him. He reminded Jack of a raccoon.

"Hey, buddy." Jack cringed as he spoke. "How's it hangin'?"

Karl drove the tip of his boot into Jack's side. Then, he did it three more times. Each successive blow, while lessened by the Kevlar vest, still hurt immensely, though Jack acted as if they hurt even worse. It was unconventional, for sure, but Jack knew what he was doing. He was allowing Karl to kick his ass. For Jack's *surprise* to work, he needed to buy it a few more minutes. He needed to buy himself some time too. If they were busy beating on him, then they were too distracted to kill him. What better way to preoccupy your enemy than to be their punching bag?

Jack broke out into a fit of coughs—real ones.

Emma's left hand rose. The nonverbal order immediately halted Karl's feverous retribution. She leaned over Jack, hands on her knees, and smiled wide at his bruised and beaten form.

Jack's lip was bleeding. He could also feel his right eye getting puffy. Even a few of his teeth felt loose. Still, he was alive, and he wasn't actually in as bad of shape as his enemies thought he was. Yes, Jack hurt like a son of a bitch, but no, he wasn't entirely out of it.

Slowly, he rolled on his side and casually lifted his left arm, pretending to shield his face. He was, in reality, checking his watch. It was cracked, but it was running. He also spotted his bracelet again, recalling something Bull had said about them.

Strength and courage are essential to a warrior because of blah, blah, blah. Jack rolled his eyes. *Yeah, Bull, I know, I know...*

"Oh, Jaaack," Emma cooed, "what have you been up to?"

He was *this close* to telling her that he had freed her hostages, if only to piss her off, but he thought better of it and kept his mouth shut. If she became aware of her men's defeat, she might decide to abandon her plan. That meant Jack would no longer be needed. It wasn't like him to think of only himself. Still, he knew it was time to save his own skin. To do that, Emma needed to continue to operate business as usual.

"I tried to reach the surface, but was cut off," Jack lied. "I've got to hand it to you, Emma. Your goons know what they're doing—except for Karl, of course. He's got shit for brains." The man huffed in anger but didn't attack. "They—" A cold droplet of water fell from somewhere above Jack and slapped him in the forehead. He focused his attention on the cave ceiling. The drip had come from directly above him, originating from the largest stalactite in the room. I reminded him of the drip back at the train station. "They, uh," he said, merging back into the conversation, "they drove me back into the bunker and resealed the wall."

Both Schmidts beamed with pride. As far as they knew, their men were heroes. It was exactly what Jack needed them to think. He was still useful to them as a hostage. Luckily for him, they didn't get the chance to re-cuff his wrists.

The subterranean explosion was deafening. It shook the treasure room hard, toppling the thirty-foot-tall statue of Julius Caesar and dislodging several enormous stalactites from the ceiling. With a thunderous crack, the one above Jack's head broke free and fell like a bomb. Emma, Gunter, Karl, and Jurgen all snapped their attention skyward and then quickly dove away.

The distraction gave Jack the chance to jump to his feet. He sprinted toward the train and leapt through the gap in between the third and fourth cars. Clearing the couplers with ease, Jack stumbled as he landed on the other side of the platform. He peeked at the tunnel entrance and watched as thousands of pounds of stone collapsed in on itself, blocking the way back to Auschwitz. His surprise had worked.

It may have worked 'too' well.

Jack headed straightaway for the nearest artery into the maze of treasure, collecting a hefty Templar shield on his way in. Bullets tore into the ground all around him. He cumbersomely angled the shield behind him and was happy to see it take the forceful impacts with nothing more than a series of *bongs* and a jumble of circular indentions. The sight made him smile on the inside. He had just effectively blocked modern-day automatic gunfire with an eight-hundred-year-old instrument of defense. He sort of felt like Captain America.

If only I could heal as fast as that guy.

Jack zigged and zagged, desperately making an effort to lose his hunters. Out of breath, he stopped, hands on his knees. Heaving heavily, Jack tried to come up with a plan on the spot but couldn't.

He was too tired for his mind to focus that intensely. So, instead, he searched for something to defend himself with. Jack turned and—

"Oh."

It was the same accumulation of weapons that he'd found the Persian scimitar inside of. Jack dove into the pile and drew the first armament he laid his hands on, an exquisite Japanese katana. He hurriedly drew the sword from its sheath. "Woah," Jack said, gawking at the razor-sharp, steel blade. It was flawless, expertly engraved with a dragon that was inlaid with gold. The katana's handle was also intricately designed, as was its sheath.

Japanese weaponry wasn't Jack's forte, but he did recall that the greatest bladesmith in the nation's history was supposed to have lived around the same time as the Knights Templar.

I wonder if this is one of Masamune's creations.

The answer to his question would have to wait. Footsteps erupted nearby. Even though Jack was *armed*—more or less—he didn't stick around to fight anyone head-on with only a sword and shield. He ran and came upon something else familiar, scrambling up-and-over a voluminous sea of hardbacks and paperbacks.

He stumbled his way to the peak before he was discovered. Before he could celebrate his successful summiting, a barrage of gunfire forced him to dive forward. Careful not to land on his sword, Jack aimed for his downward turned shield. He rode it head-first like a reckless teen on a toboggan, using the stone footpath between two other enormous treasure mounds as an escape route. Sparks flew up all around him while he desecrated the priceless Templar artifact. The path dead-ended at a vast mountain of coins.

His abrupt arrival caught Jurgen off-guard. Jack reacted first and swiped his katana sideways across the gunman's mid-section. He continued past the German and obliterated the once-rugged barricade that had kept the coins at bay for centuries.

Typically, someone wearing a Kevlar vest would've been safe from a common blade strike. But Jack's sword wasn't just some punk's switchblade. Also, he had aimed low and found flesh.

Jurgen showed off his inhuman toughness and tried to bring up his rifle even though he'd been mortally injured him. Jack reacted quickly and leapt to his feet, slashing his blade sideways across the mercenary's throat.

Eyes wide, Jurgen dropped his carbine and clutched his unprotected throat and gut as blood gushed from both wounds. As the mercenary stumbled away, Jack went for his felled HK416. He also relieved the struggling man of his loaded pistol and two extra, fully loaded magazines. Jack felt like a heartless pirate. Stealing the possessions of a dying man felt wrong. It was a despicable act.

As payment for his wretched behavior, the massif of coins leaned forward and buried him. Fortunately, for Jack, the loot was lighter than the books had been, and unlike the tempest of tomes, the coins filled in all the available space around his body. He held his breath and didn't fight the swarm. Instead, he allowed it to envelope him.

Then, the world went dark.

Seconds later, Jack heard someone scream.

He stayed submerged for as long as he could. In the meantime, he took in small amounts of metal-tinged air. There wasn't a lot of oxygen available to him, but there was enough for him to stay submerged beneath the pile until the area around him returned to a state of silence.

Minutes passed before Jack dared to move. When he did, the gilded blanket shifted with him. It grated at his ears, sounding like thousands of pieces of sandpaper on steel. He was forced to stop and listen multiple times, too paranoid about ripping it off like a Band-Aid so he could move out. There was no telling who could be waiting for him to emerge.

His right eye, ear, and temple were the first parts to clear.

Emma's voice echoed around the chamber. Gunter called out from somewhere farther away. They were still looking for Jack. His decision to conceal himself for as long as he did was paying off. They had no idea where he was.

It won't last, Jack thought, fully emerging. Eventually, they'd circle around to this spot and find him.

He gathered his equally buried katana and rifle and stretched his lower back. Looking around, he found the bloodied mercenary thirty feet to his right. Jurgen was lying on his side in an expanding pool of crimson. Jack slid the blade back into its sheath and then slipped it in between his belt and his jeans. Shouldering the carbine, he stepped around the viscous plasma and locked onto the German's still, lifeless eyes. He had died quickly.

He regretted Jurgen's demise, not because it was by his hand, but because it could've been avoided altogether. Emma was, indeed, to blame, though these men had knowingly followed her to hell. People like this understood the risks involved.

Stop feeling sorry for the bad guys!

Emma and Gunter's voices picked up again, but this time, they were somewhere nearby. Jack rushed forward and searched Jurgen's body and did his best not to pay attention to his still face. Jack grumbled when he didn't find any additional rifle magazines.

"Sorry 'bout this pal," Jack said, standing. "I really am."

He was about to strip the man's pack off his back but was stopped by a nearby shout. Jack sighed and got to his feet, knowing what needed to be done. Emma wasn't going to give up and throw down her weapons and surrender. She, and what was left of her team, were prepared to fight until the bitter end and die here—today.

Emma's world was falling apart all around her. Jurgen was dead, eviscerated by a man she should've killed from the onset. Jack's explosive charges had collapsed the entry tunnel, cutting off all communication to the outside world. As far as she knew, there was no other way back to the surface except to keep moving forward and see where the tracks would take them.

Himmler's journal referred to a veiled exit somewhere en route to the Owl Mountains, but he had purposely left it vague enough so that the location couldn't be found. If he had just come out and revealed it, then this place, Emma's fortune, would've been discovered long ago.

Emma's parents were well-off financially. They had no interest in finding the train despite their family history. When she was young, she'd bring up the mysterious haul out of sheer childhood curiosity. Her mother and father would only shake their heads and scoff at the idea of spending their money to *maybe* find more. Emma was lucky—blessed even—to have grown up in an affluent household.

Presently, she didn't feel lucky or blessed. She felt cursed.

A single human being was ruining years of preparation in mere hours. Was her plan so poorly prepared, or was Jack Reilly that good? Emma wasn't the least bit egotistical. She could admit that both were true. They had horribly underestimated the American from the get-go. She'd done it again when she'd brought him along as an insurance policy. Emma could've brought one of the meeker civilians along instead, but Jack's knowledge of the subject made her more eager to bring him. His presence had severely clouded her judgment—so had the prospect of dragging a former Special Forces soldier around like a dog.

Maybe her ego was out of control? Even now, she needed to stop believing everything would be okay. She needed to start treating Jack as if he was a viable threat—because he was. But that didn't mean Emma couldn't come up with a way to neutralize him.

"Regroup!" she shouted in German. "Back to the train, now!"

17

Ten minutes had passed since Jack had heard Emma's shouts. Since then, the treasure room had been consumed by an eerie stillness. It gave Jack the willies. At this point, he'd rather have the room filled with screams and gunfire. At least he would know where the others were.

"What are you up to?" Jack quietly asked, visualizing the German radicals. To him, the scampering trio would look like cockroaches diving underneath a refrigerator in response to the kitchen light turning on.

And I'm their exterminator.

Jack was making his way straight for the unexplored exit tunnel—the one the train was facing. He stopped just outside of the archway, ducking behind a beautifully carved statue of the seated Hindu deity, Shiva. On one knee, Jack readied his rifle, lying in wait for someone to appear. He planned to shoot and kill anyone he saw. There'd be no prisoners. He was past that. It was an unpleasant ultimatum, but in actuality, it was his only option.

His idea was foolproof too. There was no way back to Auschwitz. The only way out of the treasure room was back through the passage to the Templar temple, but even it didn't contain a serviceable exit.

Except for door number three, maybe. It was the only path he'd yet to explore.

There was a chance, with the proper climbing gear, that Jack could make it up the cliff face beneath where he had fallen through the tracks. It would be a problematic trek—one he'd attempt if it were his only option—though, he had a feeling there were secondary outlets somewhere between the chamber and wherever the tracks ended. The Nazis had been brutish in most of their ways, but they had also proven to be exceptional engineers. Everything beneath Auschwitz was evidence of that. It would've been a grade school mistake not to cut hidden access points along the way.

He eyed the tunnel and, once more, just for a moment, thought about sneaking off. If there was a secondary exit nearby, he could, at the very least, get help and come back with reinforcements.

"Come on, Jack," he said, shaking his head, "you know you can't do that."

He wasn't about to let Emma, Gunter, and Karl slip away so easily. If he did, there was a chance Emma would ultimately get what she wanted. A new Reich, along with a modernized Schutzstaffel, would rise to power with a literal fortune to fund them. Moreover, Emma was smart. She wouldn't try to overtake a government from the outside. She'd use her vast wealth to cleverly manipulate things from within. Policies and laws were the contemporary weapons of government. Amend them, in just the right way, and you could allow anyone to do anything—and it'd be legal.

That terrified Jack.

He was a retired soldier, not a politician. He fought because he believed in it, not because he expected something grand in return. Like now, the only thing Jack wanted was to keep one of the world's greatest enemies from being resurrected.

I'd like to live too.

Movement behind the train engine caught his eye. It was challenging to identify the shadowy person, though after watching the individual for a few seconds, he could tell that it was Emma and not one of her male associates. Her silhouette was shaped differently.

If Jack popped up and took the shot, he was sure he'd be able to hit her. But if he did, he'd be putting himself in a dangerous situation. He'd be out in the open with two other shooters on the loose.

Emma paced back and forth, looking very frustrated. Eventually, she paused, facing the other direction. The woman was staring at something in the first row of riches. The whole scene felt odd. It felt forced. She was baiting Jack to reveal himself!

"Well," he said, "I'd hate to disappoint her."

But, he did.

Jack but on the brakes and forced himself to stay put. Finally, after ninety excruciating seconds, Emma glanced over her shoulder and spoke to someone that was out of sight. Jack's reservations had been warranted. There was another person close by. If he had leapt into action, instead of staying vigilant, he'd have been killed.

Hmmm, he thought, deciding what to do next.

He turned and leaned his back against the base of Shiva's statue and looked up, seeing something he liked. The passage leading back to the Templar church was just barely in sight. If he could lead Emma and the others into the tunnels, he'd be able to play by his own rules. Jack had only been in them for a short time before, but he was confident that he knew them better than the others. At this juncture, it was a sound plan because heading into the exit without knowing what waited was worse.

A second tunnel collapse, perhaps? Snakes and bears? It could be anything after eight decades of human inactivity.

Ducking away, Jack crouch-ran back up the sloping incline, moving as fast as he could without making too much noise. He zigged left around seven ornately carved Roman chariots, and a column of two dozen Chinese terracotta soldiers. Then, he zagged right around a quartet of beautifully preserved stone statues.

Jack made it up to the uppermost pathway before his foot slipped and kicked a handful pebbles down the trail. Bullets pinged all around him as he dove to the ground. Luckily, there was plenty of cover, and he quickly popped up to his hands and knees and scurried away. Both he and the gunfire halted when he entered the corridor. He could've kept going, but he needed his adversaries to follow him.

"Missed me!" he called out, leaping to his feet. He waved at Emma, who could just be seen leaning out from behind the train engine. "Come and get me, assholes!"

More bullets were sent flying his way, but Jack was already on the move. He flicked on his rifle's light and took the passage as fast as he could. The spiraling waterfall staircase was next. The slickening spray forced Jack to slow down. He lost sight of his entry point as he passed beneath each of the waterfalls. Each time he re-exposed himself, he leveled his carbine up at the tunnel, expecting someone to be aiming one back at him.

With one more waterfall to go, he slid to a stop. Emma, Gunter, and Karl all poured out of the corridor and went about clearing the immediate area. There was a twenty-foot expanse of nothing between Jack and the lower level's tunnel. If he stayed put behind the dense wall of water, he'd be safe until they got nearer to his position.

"This would've been a lot easier seven-hundred years ago."

At worst, he'd have faced a bow and arrow. Other than that, every attack would've been from up close, something Jack knew he could handle. Bullets, however, were much harder to dodge than sword blades.

He checked his rifle's ammo and found that he only had nine rounds left. Luckily, he still had his Glock and a considerable number of spare rounds. He'd yet to use the sidearm since he appropriated it from Jurgen.

Edging out to his left, toward the exit, Jack spied Emma as she slipped behind the uppermost waterfall. Gunter and Karl were nowhere to be seen. He figured the two men were already on the way to him, moving off while the water still shielded Jack.

"Right..."

Shouldering his carbine, Jack sidestepped left and aimed for the opposite side of the cascading water. Carefully, he took each step, descending sideways. Halfway to his goal, he calmly squeezed the trigger three times when he saw movement.

Emma. And he had *just* missed.

Two figures popped out from the next waterfall further down the staircase. Gunter and Karl had moved past the first one without Jack knowing, and once more, had used Emma as bait. Jack unloaded the rest of his magazine, before tossing the spent rifle into the surging water.

He drew his pistol, lifted his arms in front of him, and backed into the tight corridor just as two projectiles embedded themselves into his vest. The impact, along with the slick footing, caused Jack to stagger and fall. He tumbled down the narrow stairwell, feeling every bump and bruise from the last time he'd fallen down a flight of stairs. Gratefully, the steps here weren't overly steep, and he stopped a few rolls later. Swiftly, Jack got to his feet, holding his side.

"Ow."

Activating his Glock's tactical light, Jack pushed forward, breathing heavily. The lower ribs in his left side throbbed. He'd taken both rounds off-center of his gut. It felt like he'd gotten kicked in the stomach by a mule.

He was so focused on his physical state that he didn't notice that he had just entered the circular, three-story living space. The tunnel straight ahead led back into the church. The path to his right led to the broken suspension bridge—a route that was, presumably, still currently blocked by the massive rectangular-cut stone.

The only other option was the tunnel to his left, door number three. He'd yet to explore it, though. Jack pointed his gun light into it and saw nothing but darkness at the end of the beam. If he had more time, he'd take a quick look and see where it led before committing to it. Time, however, was something he didn't have.

A soft breeze buffeted his face. Air flowed from the left-hand tunnel, swooped through, and funneled back toward the cylindrical chamber with the waterfalls.

It gave him an idea.

Jack holstered his sidearm and turned on his chest-mounted, right-angle light. He quickly scooped up as much of the hay as he could, dropping all of it just outside the mouth of the passageway. Then, he carefully lifted one of the chair's charred legs and jammed it deep inside the mound of fresh bedding.

He knelt and fueled the embers, blowing softly, happy it lit without trouble. As he had hoped, the smoke was directed forward into the corridor. He redrew his pistol and backed away, keeping its light extinguished. The growing firelight was plenty to see by. He tipped over a nearby table and got into place behind it. It wasn't going to stop any bullets, but it would at least conceal his exact position.

The only chink in his plan was *time*. Time always won. If Emma and the others took too much of it to get there, the fire and smoke would die down. Still, Jack needed to try and hold the line. He raised his Glock and set the barrel on the inverted table's edge, using it as a tripod of sorts. His aim would be precise. Without it, he wasn't sure if he could hit the broadside of a barn. He was too damn tired. Squinting against the firelight and the noxious miasma, Jack thought he saw movement on the other side of the flames. He slowly took in the slack of the trigger and paused. There, on its *wall*, he waited for confirmation. An ill-advised shot would give away his intentions.

Wait for a clear target, he thought.

At least his foes wouldn't be able to shoot back at him while inside the tight confines of the tunnel unless they didn't care about the health of their eardrums. That was a real-life danger and something that wasn't brought up in movies very often, at all. Even now, Jack's headache came from being underground while shooting a gun. That, and the multiple blows to his skull.

And, just like that, his cover was decimated by semi-automatic gunfire. Wooden shrapnel was thrown into his face and body as he covered his head and rolled away from the barrage. Somehow, Jack wasn't struck by a single round as he inched away, slinking across the stone floor like a worm. He retreated into the unexplored passage and shambled to his feet. Doing something stupid, he fired his pistol behind him, and as he expected, the sound was deafening—literally. A Mike Tyson-like haymaker to the brain followed each trigger pull. The pain was beyond excruciating.

Death would be worse, Jack thought, gritting his teeth. *Death would be so much worse.*

18

Jack blinked hard, trying desperately to push aside the agony in his head and the ringing in his ears. It was like a flashbang had gone off nearby. For all intents and purposes, his plan was a complete and utter bust. His pursuers had blown away his expectations every step of the way. He honestly figured that they would let him re-enter the tunnels and leave him be since he was a secondary piece to the puzzle.

"Nope, wrong!" he shouted in frustration, barely hearing his own words. It had sounded like he screamed underwater. Clicking on his pistol light, he checked his surroundings.

Presently, Emma wanted him dead as much as she desired her fortune. Jack had made himself a part of her mission ever since he killed Jurgen and collapsed the tunnel leading back to Auschwitz, which was more than likely already crawling with cops—military too. It wasn't just a local business that had gotten taken over by a local gang. One of the most famous places on planet Earth had been occupied by terrorists.

Jack was amazed by how far he had traveled thus far. The passageway directly behind him—the one with the broken suspension bridge—ended abruptly. This one went on forever. It made things worse for him. He needed to keep Emma and the others close enough for them to want to pursue him, but not close enough to put two rounds in his back.

Pausing, Jack placed his hands on his hips and sucked in a handful of deep breaths. He turned and looked behind him and was *happy* to see a bouncing spot of light further back. At least one of them was following him. Dividing and conquering his foe might still be in the cards, after all, unless they were moving in a single file line.

The voice of Obi-Wan Kenobi echoed in his head. *"Sand people always ride single file, to hide their numbers."*

He moved off and kept his pace steady. Every few yards, he looked back to confirm that he was still being hunted.

A familiar noise picked up somewhere ahead. It was one he had heard before—a sound that he dreaded. The white noise was met with a wet air that could only come from one source.

"Friggin wonderful," Jack said, slowing.

Further ahead, the tunnel opened into a yawning expanse. It was similar to the cave with the busted suspended deck bridge, except it was twice the size. Happily, this gap still contained a bridge. It was an impressive display of architecture, and looked original in appearance, except for a couple of more recent additions.

The Nazis had found this and repaired it.

The bridge sagged toward the middle, like most bridges of its design and weight. Hip-high, feeble-looking railings ran along either side of it too. It looked incredibly similar to the one from *Indiana Jones and the Temple of Doom.* Hopefully, there weren't any crocodiles below.

Jack leaned out over the drop and aimed his weapon light down. He lost the bottom of it somewhere in the shadows and spray. The sound of rushing water was booming. Even with his ears ringing and muffled from the earlier gunfight, he could hear it. He swept his light left and right and saw that the void went on for quite some distance. This wasn't an isolated chasm.

"Now, that's one big ass hole."

Focusing on the bridge itself, he stepped out onto the first plank and froze when it creaked beneath his weight.

"Not a chance," he said, finding another option.

To the right of the mouth of the tunnel was a short ledge that traveled ten feet out onto the cliff face. It was a natural formation and one he'd use to spring a trap on whoever was following him. He prayed it was just one of either Emma, Gunter, or Karl and not all three of them.

Jack had a feeling it would be Karl. He was the low man left on the totem pole and a man that Jack had, admittedly, rubbed up the wrong way on several occasions. After some time to reflect, stripping Karl naked was probably a bad idea and the last straw. Not only had Jack consistently annoyed the psychopath, but he had also embarrassed him.

The ledge quickly went from a foot in depth down to less than four inches. The heels of Jack's sneakers did their best to find purchase. He slipped on the slick stone twice. Once he was in position, he shut off his light, holstered his weapon, and waited. He didn't want to risk losing his firearm if, and when, he was forced to defend himself.

If felt like a lifetime had gone by before he heard anything. It was faint too, but it was there. The rushing water mostly drowned out everything except the blood pulsing through his skull. His headache had gotten bad.

He held his breath as a soft aura of light appeared from the tunnel. It grew brighter and brighter as its owner continued forward, and just when Jack was about to pounce, the beam went out. The world around Jack was thrown into total darkness once more.

What are you—

Suddenly, a light bloomed to life. It hit him directly in his dilated pupils, sucker-punching him in his already pounding mind. He winced but didn't slink away from it.

He did quite the contrary.

Jack launched himself across the ledge and grabbed the person's gun hand, driving it skyward. The shot went high and caused both Jack and his assailant to duck their heads in response. It was the only time Jack was thankful for being mostly deaf. In the wavering weapon light, Jack got a glimpse of the pistol's owner.

Karl's reaction was more painful looking than his. It allowed Jack to backhand the German's hand away. He followed that by driving his palm into Karl's face, stumbling him back some. Jack advanced and snagged the pistol with his left hand, depressing the gun light's power button. Everything went dark, and when it did, Jack did what he promised to do.

He wouldn't stop.

Drawing his sidearm, Jack aimed at where he last saw Karl. He squeezed the trigger, and in the flash of the firing projectile, he saw that his adversary had moved back toward the tunnel.

This time, Karl was the aggressor. He leapt inside Jack's reach, and grabbed his wrist, pushing his pistol up. Jack followed suit and wrapped his left hand around Karl's right wrist, the one holding the gun, and squeezed. Both men pushed hard, but it was a stalemate.

For now.

Jack's body screamed, protesting and complaining. He was in far worse shape than Karl, and he needed to change the status quo before the German altered it himself.

Taking a step backward, Jack allowed Karl to guide him toward the bridge. Three such steps later, Karl joined Jack on the creaking, ancient structure. As it bent and flexed beneath their moving feet, it also swayed slightly. Karl pulled the trigger of his pistol and grinned when Jack reflexively flinched. His face morphed into a full-fledged smile as he slowly turned the barrel toward Jack's face.

In the darkness, right then and there, Jack looked down. He visualized what was directly below his feet, picturing the water beneath him meeting up with the river he'd been in twice before—twice more than he would've preferred. All of the subterranean tributaries seemed to converge in the same place, back where he had first fallen through the elevated tracks. That knowledge gave Jack an advantage, but it also presented him a horrible idea, and if he didn't act fast, he'd lose the battle. He could feel his strength rapidly diminishing.

Karl released Jack's gun hand and smashed his left fist into his foe's face. Woozy, Jack tried and failed to raise his pistol and pull the trigger. His head swam.

Swam...

"Hey, Karl..." Jack said, his vision dancing, "can you swim?"

Jack leaned right and went limp. Two-hundred pounds of dead weight rapidly brought the unbalanced, unsuspecting German along for the ride. Jack's hip bumped the low rail. Underneath the men's combined mass, it cracked and abruptly rocked the rope bridge. They spilled over the rail and fell into nothingness.

Gunshots spewed wildly as the pair struggled to shoot the other. With each successive gunshot, Jack could see Karl's snarling, bestial face. The roar of a raging river rose to a crescendo, and just before Jack plunged through its surface for a third time, he released his hold on Karl's gun hand and took a deep breath.

The Glock was nearly knocked away from him by one of Karl's flailing appendages. But all the blow did was activate Jack's weapon light. The pair plunged beneath the surging rapids. The cold temperature snapped Jack back into focus, awakening what must be his fourth or fifth wind.

Within the swirling illumination, Jack reacquired Karl—not that pulling the trigger while submerged would do a damn thing. The first thing he noticed was the look on the big German's face. Karl no longer looked like he wanted to kill Jack. He looked surprised. Jack was likewise confused until his light's beam turned red. Karl's line of sight dropped to his own chest.

Jack followed the man's eyes. There were twin holes in his exposed sternum. Jack was currently wearing Karl's protective vest—a garment that would've stopped the bullets from entering the other man's body.

The water ushered both men along, separating them for a moment, then crashing them back into one another seconds later. Jack drove his feet into Karl. With not delay, he shoved, and kicked him away.

Pointing his light forward, Jack angled his body like a torpedo and allowed the river to direct him. The underground channel was as craggy as the others but more open. And like before, the ceiling above his head disappeared without notice. Jack was bowled into from behind. Startled, he lost most of his held oxygen in a burst of bubbles. Apparently, Karl wasn't down for the count.

Jack was belly-up with Karl directly atop him. Both men rode the current like a pair of synchronized dolphins. While Karl focused on choking the life out of Jack, the former Delta operator was paying attention to his surroundings. The ceiling was rapidly appearing and disappearing overhead. If Jack could time its reappearance correctly...

There!

Jack slid his arms in between their bodies, and he heaved Karl upward, wincing when the man's face cracked against a jagged outcrop of rock. It missed Jack's nose by inches, nearly dislodging his gun from his numb hands. In desperate need of air, Jack pushed away from the ceiling and turned over. The current rolled him around to the left, and the passage narrowed slightly.

It opened into a swirling vortex of water. When it did, Jack kicked to the surface and took in a deep breath. He felt around for his thigh holster, slipping his pistol inside before it was torn away.

The light wasn't powerful enough to see anything of use, but Jack knew where he was. He was back under the tracks, where the main tributaries converged. The earlier idea of climbing the cliff was quickly swept away—as was Jack. Like he had twice before, the waterfall threw Jack into the air. He curled into a ball and re-entered the water and rode the bumpy water ride back to the glassy Templar pool.

Jack surfaced, treading water for a moment. He caught his breath and doggy paddled over to the bank. He pulled himself up and flopped onto the flat stone and laid still, staring up at the ceiling. In the silent, calm of the cave, he was startled when something else entered behind him.

Staying down, Jack rolled onto his left side and drew his pistol, activating its light. He acquired the latest threat, though, it wasn't a *new* enemy. It was a very familiar one, and he was floating face down, unmoving.

Jack waited twenty seconds before getting to his feet. He kept his gun leveled at the buoyant man and crept up to the bank's edge. After an additional ten seconds of inaction, Jack turned away.

Karl was dead.

Drenched, yet again, Jack shook it off and depressed his Glock's magazine release and checked his ammo. Satisfied, he replaced it inside the weapon's handgrip, holstered it, and stepped away.

"Right," he muttered, holding his bruised ribs. "Now for Emma and Gunter."

19

The Schmidts took cover the way Jack had done and knelt behind an overturned table. They both had their weapons drawn and aimed down the tunnel, waiting for either Karl or Jack to emerge. Gunter doubted both men would return. Karl went in knowing that there was a chance he wouldn't see any of his comrades again.

"I will make you proud," he had said, turning and stomping away.

The fire to Emma and Gunter's left had died down. It was a clever move on Jack's part to think of it so quickly. Unfortunately, for the American, they were already a step ahead of him. Lying near their feet were four small wads of torn fabric. They had used the material as earplugs to muffle the concussive sound of their weapons while firing them in the tight confines of the subterranean corridors. The abusive report didn't get completely suppressed, but it worked well enough.

Emma and Gunter waited for their friend for ten minutes. Agitated, Emma stood and stepped around the table.

"Emma!" Gunter hissed.

She shot her brother a venomous glare, silencing him without a word. Biting his lip, he stood and followed her, keeping an eye on their rear. The American had proved wily. The setting, and the man's unwillingness to die, spooked the otherwise stoic mercenary. Few had ever made Gunter feel this way.

He respected Jack.

"We must take great care," he said softly.

Emma ignored him. She was lost in her rage, blindly focused on killing the man that was responsible for ruining her years of planning. Yes, Jack Reilly needed to die, but Gunter was worried that his sister's foolish mindset would make her fall in the process. He loved Emma, but she was her own woman. Gunter could only do so much to protect her. But...

Sorry, Emma, he thought. *If it comes to it, I'm choosing my life over Jack's death.*

The trail was straight and true, and it didn't rise or fall. The construction was impossibly precise. The duo marched on in silence until they heard water. The suspension bridge was something to behold, as was the expanse of the chasm. It was tranquil, and it bothered Gunter terribly.

Neither Karl nor Jack were present.

"You think they went across?" he asked.

Emma didn't reply, and she didn't stop. Without testing the bridge's structural integrity, Emma continued forward, locked in, and zoned out. Gunter waited for his sister to reach the halfway point before following. When she did, he stepped as she did—where she did. A few feet out and to his left, Gunter noticed that a section of the railing was badly damaged. The breakage didn't seem to weaken the bridge in the least, though. He didn't stick around long enough to see if it was a new break or not.

Emma moved quicker as she neared the other side. The bridge was sound all the way across. In his weapon light, Gunter watched Emma enter the tunnel and hurry inside, never once looking back.

Before following her, Gunter paused and faced the other way, shining his light across the expanse. He held it, and his breath, and waited. When no one emerged, he exhaled, turned, and crossed the threshold.

Jack stayed hidden until Gunter was out of sight. After climbing up to the second floor of the Templar church, he had hightailed it to the circular living quarters, glad to find it deserted. Jack was correct to assume that Emma and her brother would go to check on Karl. If he decided wrong, then it was apparent that they headed back to the treasure room instead.

Regrettably, Jack was now at level ground with his foes. He had no idea what lay ahead. Returning to the train was a possibility, for sure. If he did, he could spring a trap and take the Schmidts out together. He thought it over and decided to go with his gut and stepped back onto the decking of the suspension bridge.

Gunter had only just vanished further underground. Still, Jack needed to hang back and be cautious. If they suspected that he was following them, they could turn the tides quickly.

The trek across the bridge started out fine, but then Jack came across the portion that he and Karl had damaged. As soon as his left foot came down, the bridge listed in that direction, and his knee gave out. Luckily, Jack caught himself, and he didn't spill back into the raging river below.

But his gun did.

"Well, shit..." he said, watching the illuminated weapon flip end over end until—*sploosh*—gone.

With his only real means of defending himself now sleeping with the fishes, Jack unsheathed the German trench knife he had begun his journey with. It was the only armament he had left. With no light to see by, Jack patted himself down and felt something in one of the pockets on his vest. Reaching in, he was happy to find six glow sticks. He removed one and cracked it, shaking it vigorously. The *Sharpie*-sized object glowed orange and settled a little of Jack's rising anxiety. Regardless, he proceeded by stepping slowly and felt each section of decking for weak spots.

Arriving at the other end, Jack knelt just outside the passage and waited. He shielded the glow stick and couldn't see squat—which was great. It meant that he was alone—or at least—that's what he was hoping for.

Jack stood and transferred the glow stick into his knife hand, holding both together. Next, he felt for the ceiling, finding it a foot above his head. He kept his empty hand on its surface and carefully proceeded forward, using it as a guide. Jack gripped the trench knife's hilt and the glow stick tightly, covering the light the best he could. With no gun, Jack was at a serious disadvantage and needed to resort to stealth over force.

Soft, muted voices beckoned him onward. A dozen steps later, he emerged and quickly found cover behind a thick stalagmite near the outskirts of another impressive cavern. He pocketed the glow stick and leaned out, spotting a ring of several more orange chemiluminescences off in the distance. They encompassed the center of the room, and within their collective aura, stood Emma and Gunter.

Jack estimated the cavern to be somewhere between two and three hundred feet in diameter. The floor of the cave was mostly clear apart from a pair of enormous, naturally formed columns, as well as a handful of small depressions filled with mineral-laced water, the lifeblood of the rock formations.

The Schmidts stood with their backs to him, pointing their flashlights at a lump on the floor. Jack was too far away to tell what it was that held their attention. Emma knelt and covered her mouth with one hand. Her other hand was pressed up against her chest. It was a display of emotion, one that seemed out of character. He had seen very little of that from Emma since meeting her. Whatever they'd found, it must've been something amazing to behold.

Jack needed to see it too.

Few things could move a person as heartless as Emma Schmidt. If it brought her to her knees, then it would blow Jack's socks off for sure. Even Gunter was taken aback by it. Considering their family history and the reason they were here, Jack thought it was safe to assume that it was somehow Nazi related.

He waited an agonizing fifteen minutes before Emma and Gunter headed back the way they had come. Jack's eyes opened wide, and he looked for somewhere to hide. With no other option, he hugged close to the spire of stone and prayed he wouldn't be found. Emma wasn't carrying a weapon, but Gunter was. He still held his rifle at the low-ready, head on a swivel.

Jack couldn't chance it.

Keeping the column between him and the Schmidts, Jack crept sideways, cringing with every step he took. At their closest, Emma and Gunter passed within ten feet of Jack's hiding spot. The stone spike was barely thick enough to conceal him, but it did the job. Plus, Jack hadn't given them a reason to think that he had followed them.

As they reentered the passage back up to the Templar caves, Jack wiped his brow and quietly made his way over to the center of the room. The glow sticks still had plenty of juice left in them. The lighting wasn't the problem. The issue with what he saw was coming to terms with what it was, or rather, who *he* was.

Like Emma, Jack knelt and got a closer look.

The first thing he noted was the man's clothing—his uniform. Even after eight decades of grime, Jack recognized him as a high-ranking Nazi officer. However, it was the man's matching collar insignias that gave his identity away. The historians had gotten this one wrong. He hadn't killed himself like they had said, at least, not while he was in British custody anyway.

"Heinrich Himmler."

The Reichsfuhrer of Hitler's Schutzstaffel was here—in the flesh—sort of. It's why Emma had been so broken up about it. Lying here was a man she still idolized. Seeing the body in front of him, Jack realized that perhaps Himmler had escaped the Allies and had died down here, maybe even on his own terms. Inspecting him further, Jack couldn't see the back of Himmler's head and body, but the sight was too much to take in and he knew it had been hard for Emma to handle.

It dawned on Jack that he had once read an article describing how most of the Nazi commanders had professional stand-ins. The lookalikes had known everything there was to know about their twin. And Jack was sure Himmler would have had help from German spies on the inside. They had been everywhere back then. It would have been easy for the Allies to have captured Himmler's double, who would have been able to keep up the rouse, while the real Himmler got away.

"And you came here." He looked around and pictured everything he'd seen since stepping foot into the Death Block.

Medical records would have been a cinch to alter. Nothing had been digital and paper copies would've needed to have been accessed and swapped out. It may have even been done years before the war ended, but Jack was just guessing.

Did that mean that Hitler may have survived too? His death had been a suspicious one. Like Himmler, Hitler had, supposedly, killed himself. What had never added up was that the bullet had entered through his forehead, an odd angle to have shot one's self. It would have been more plausible had it been done under the chin or into the temple, which was more common in firearm-related suicides. Some theorists have said that Hitler, or maybe his body double, had been murdered and then staged to look like a suicide. And again, Hitler's medical records could have been easily modified.

It made sense to Jack why Himmler had come here. There were plenty of supplies, and few knew of the bunker's existence. And he would have needed a secure place to hide. He had been responsible for a lot, not more than Hitler himself, but he easily took second place. Few had ever held an office as powerful and influential as Himmler. There was only one other person Jack could compare him to. General Erwin Rommel, commander of the German Army's Afrika Corps.

Himmler had returned here for something that he valued.

"The treasure," Jack whispered, standing. He never took his eyes off the corpse. "You came back for the treasure, didn't you? Probably right after Adolf offed himself."

If that's what really happened.

It terrified Jack to think there was a world where Hitler, Himmler, and Josef Mengele had all gotten away. The Nazi physician had somehow outrun the law for years, most notably Israeli Mossad agents. Thankfully, for all of humankind, it looked as if the other two had died, either just before the war ended, or shortly thereafter. Just because Himmler escaped custody, didn't mean Hitler had.

Jack blinked hard and refocused. He needed to stay on *this side* of paranoia. He also needed to catch up with Emma and Gunter before they too slipped away from justice. Following them would be easy, but it would also be dangerous and downright foolish. Since they had lost him, Jack didn't think they would be outright hunting him. They would still be extremely cautious, but not ravenously trying to find and kill him.

That's what he supposed, anyway.

Jack was drained. He needed a break to reset, so he pushed forward. Nature's design would lead the way. At the other end of the cave was a tall, thin pathway. Initially, he could barely squeeze through. His vest made it difficult, but once he got himself going, the passage opened enough to move about freely.

In the soft illumination of his glow stick, Jack looked up. The ceiling was veiled from sight, high over his head. The ground beneath his feet was uneven and difficult to navigate. His assessment of the trail—something Bull had taught him to do—was that it hadn't been in regular use back when people roamed these caves on a more regular basis.

Jack estimated that he had traveled about half a mile by the time he saw something different than his narrow-walled strip of tunneling. In this case, the corridor's ceiling shot down out of the heavens and cut the path's height down to three feet. Grumbling under his breath, Jack sheathed his trench knife and dropped onto his hands and knees. He shuffled forward for twenty feet before seeing something he recognized. Facing down, and with just his head sticking out, Jack saw train tracks. Next, he looked right and then left, smiling wide.

There, he saw the backside of a familiar set of handcarts. He was back at the train station, and he couldn't have been happier. Jack pulled himself up to his feet and limped toward the station. He squeezed around a duo of carts before reaching the edge of the platform. Just beyond that were the bodies they had found earlier.

Jack wanted to avoid them, if at all possible.

He reentered the cavern and saw the wheelbarrow he and Emma had found the gold coin in. It all felt like a lifetime ago. Looking up at the metal hatch, Jack thought about heading back inside and searching the weapons locker, but he doubted anything would work after eighty years of inaction. He unsheathed his knife and looked it over.

"Just you and me, little buddy."

Instead of sheathing the blade in his belt at the small of his back, Jack slid it into where Karl's tactical knife had once been. He headed for the front edge of the platform and got down onto his ass, gingerly slid off, and landed as gracefully as he could under the circumstances.

Glow stick in hand, Jack set off to confront the Schmidt siblings for what he hoped was the last time. At this point, he'd like nothing more than to get home and hug that Grizzly.

20

The treasure room was, once again, quiet. Jack made sure before rushing out, waiting until his knees were killing him. Kneeling was a pain—literally. He groaned and got to his feet and ducked inside, taking the route he had used beforehand. He slid up against the nearest sarcophagi and zeroed in on Jurgen's final resting place. Jack needed supplies, and he was hoping that the others hadn't stripped the man of anything else useful. His ammo was gone. Jack saw to that the last time.

He knelt again and leaned out. "But what about your backpack?" Inside was weeks of supplies, and water wouldn't be an issue down here. He could always make his way back to the Templar church and collect some if he needed, but that's not why he wanted Jurgen's pack. Jack wanted it for the trek home, or more accurately, his return trip to the surface. He had no idea how long it would take, and he needed to be prepared for anything.

Jack could use the man's blade too. As much as his trench knife had grown on him, the modern variation was a far-superior design.

Going uphill when your legs felt like a melting Jell-O mold was a bitch of a task, but Jack did it without too much complaining. As he talked to himself, his comments came in the form of disjointed profanities and an amalgamation of grunts and growls. Three crossroads later, Jack turned right and continued into the center portion of the collection. Jurgen was right where he had left him, and so was his fully stocked survivalist backpack, and his knife. Jack took them both. He stood and shuffled through the sea of wealth and got another idea. Throwing off his pack, he opened it and threw a few handfuls of gold coins inside.

Worst case, he could buy his way back home if he didn't get his wallet and passport back. He knew of a couple of people that could help with that—people involved in his past life. Best case, he'd set a little trap for the mad mind of the woman formerly known as Emma

Schmidt. Jack didn't know who she was now, but ever since they had discovered the treasure, she'd gone full-on psychopath. Jack could only imagine what someone who knew her better thought—someone like her brother. Gunter, even with all his anger issues, seemed like a pretty level-headed guy when he wasn't punching or kicking people, namely Jack.

It was times like this that Jack was glad to be an only child.

He went to leave but stopped. He, yet again, returned his attention to Jurgen, specifically the mercenary's soiled Kevlar vest. With no heavy weapon to drag around, Jack decided that carrying extra armor would be a good thing. If he needed to ditch it, he could, no big deal. Halfway through unbuckling it, he heard voices. Jack needed to hurry if he was to keep up his rouse. Hopefully, they thought he and Karl had died fighting one another.

He circled back around to the exit tunnel near the front of the train engine. Once there, he hid and watched to see what all of the commotion was about—not that he understood a lick of it. Emma's body language gave away her frustration, though, as did her feral cries. She had officially lost it. Gunter, on the other hand, seemed to be very much in control of himself. He stayed quiet and allowed his sister to vent.

"Smart man," Jack mumbled. "Hell hath no fury like Emma scorned."

Maybe I can use that...

He would do to Emma as he had done with Karl. He planned on using her boiling over rage against her.

"This might be really stupid," he whispered before clearing his throat. "Aw, Emma," he called out, moving as he spoke, "what's wrong, darlin'?"

"You!" she shrieked. "I'll kill you!"

Jack laughed. "You keep telling me that, yet, here I am. I'm beginning to think you might be lying."

He moved higher up into the collection and veered right. Then, he stopped and called out. "I saw Himmler, by the way!"

Jack snuck a peek and watched her. She had her pistol drawn and was death-gripping it. Gunter was still in the same spot he was before Jack had started up. He was listening, eyes closed, trying to pick up on Jack's location.

"Fat chance," he said softly, moving off again.

Emma's hands went to her head, and she somehow grabbed two fistfuls of hair, even with a gun in her hand. She was a mess.

"He was amazing, wasn't he?" she replied, through a maniacal laugh. "A true honor to be in his presence."

Jack snorted out a laugh. He wasn't sure if it was loud enough for her to hear, and he didn't stop to check. He kept going, darting right, heading back toward the rear wall—the one with the tall Greek statues.

"Yeah, he was," Jack shouted, "until I pissed down his throat!"

Gunfire erupted, but it was nowhere near where Jack was. She sent the rounds into random locations within the treasure room. Jack watched as one of the bullets took the head off a priceless terracotta soldier. He slid to a stop and noticed that Gunter was missing.

"Great..." he muttered. "Now, I have to deal with him too."

Kevlar vest around his shoulder, Jack hustled straight for the train. Emma was pacing back and forth, not too far from the fourth and fifth cars. Jack's next move was idiotic, and it would need to be timed perfectly. If it wasn't, he'd be turned into Swiss cheese.

Running downhill, Jack burst out onto the platform, instantly getting Emma's attention. She screamed and swung her pistol around to meet him. He was still a good fifty feet away, and she was still really pissed. The weapon shook horribly, even with a two-handed grip.

She fired off another four rounds his way. One impacted Jurgen's raised vest, and the others went wide. His shield properly absorbed the bullet as he had hoped, and before Emma could continue her onslaught, Jack leapt through the cars and disappeared from view. A stream of high-caliber rifle rounds nearly followed him through, smacking against the flank of the train cars. It was plain to see that

Gunter had joined the fray.

A bullet to the ass had almost undone Jack's plan.

"No!" Emma shrieked.

Jack kept the vest and slunk in between the treasure mounds on the other side. This portion wasn't as vast, but it still contained a plethora of hiding places.

"Where are you?" Jack asked himself, looking for Gunter.

"Here."

Jack turned and whipped the vest around with him. The weighty garment clipped Gunter's outstretched gun hand, and immediately, the fight turned into a brawl—a real slobber knocker. Luckily for Jack, the German didn't have his carbine anymore.

He rushed Gunter and staggered him backward for just long enough to shed his restrictive backpack. When he did, Gunter used their momentum to his advantage and pulled Jack to the ground.

Jack mimicked his fight with Karl.

He wrapped his legs around Gunter's back and locked his ankles, keeping the man in close. Then, he used a sequence of sharp elbow strikes. Except Gunter got his hands up and blocked most of them. A few of them landed, but Jack was quickly running out of steam. Soon, the blows would be closer to wet noodles slapping concrete, than disorienting headshots.

"Argh!" Jack yelped, feeling something jab his left armpit. He hadn't been stabbed, thank God, but the prod had been from something pretty sharp. It was a susceptible location, and one Jack had used to his advantage over the years. He released Gunter and kicked him away, quickly rolling to his feet. The other man stood as well, and they squared off again.

"Nice moves, *Hans*," Jack poked, rubbing the underside of his left arm. "What the hell was that?"

Gunter held up his right fist, extending the knuckle of his middle finger. It was the tool the man had used to hurt him.

Jack nodded. "Impressive."

"One could say the same about your resilience."

"Uh, thanks," Jack replied, lifting his fists. "I'm blushing."

The evenly matched duo traded blow after blow. Each close-handed strike was less effective than the one before. The fight was getting nowhere, and they both knew it.

"Are we...going to keep doing this...all night?" Jack asked, breathing hard.

Gunter was sweating profusely too. He looked just as winded as Jack, which should've been impossible considering the ass-kicking Jack had taken.

"What happened to Karl?"

Jack was taken aback by the question. He didn't expect Gunter to converse with him in the middle of a fistfight. So, Jack told him the truth—part of it, anyway.

"He drowned. We fell off the suspension bridge and went under. He hit his head and didn't make it."

Jack thought it was for the best that he didn't mention that he had also shot Karl in the chest twice and then forcibly shoved the man's head into an outcrop of jagged rock.

Gunter wasn't buying it. He squeezed his fists until the knuckles cracked. "So, you killed him?"

Jack held up his hands but held his ground. "To be fair, he tried to kill me first."

"And my men aboveground?"

Jack couldn't hide his deception. Instead of responding, he launched a wave of jabs at Gunter's eyes, nose, and throat. He also kicked at his knees and ankles too. Whatever he could do to weaken him and gain an edge, Jack did it. After a dozen such attempts, Gunter roared and threw Jack aside like he weighed nothing.

Well, that didn't work, he thought, putting his hand on the ground to push himself up. As he did, he felt something beneath his hand, something he recognized.

Gunter hauled Jack up by the shoulder straps of his Kevlar vest. While he did, Jack wrapped his fingers around Jurgen's discarded garment. With all the strength he had left, Jack shoved away from

Gunter and threw his hands into the air. The German was too busy fiddling with his knife to see what was in Jack's hands. He had taken his attention off his foe at the wrong time.

Jack forcibly slid the grubby, bloodied vest over Gunter's head and shoulders, rotating it back and forth, jamming it down as deep as he could. Jack ducked left under the German's wildly slashing blade, diving to the ground. The mercenary's pistol was right there. In one fluid motion, he scooped up the weapon, rolled to his feet, and leveled it at the back of Gunter's obscured head. Without skipping a beat, Jack pulled the trigger. The Kevlar absorbed most of the bullet's impact, but not all of it.

Gunter crumpled to the ground, unmoving. He was alive but incapacitated. Jack's hands found his knees, and he took in several deep breaths of blood-tinged air. He spat the crimson plasma away and moaned. The worst of his newest injuries was a tender nose and a gash on his chin.

He tested his nose and winced when he touched it.

Just like Karl.

Jack searched Gunter and found his personal belongings as well as six more orange glow sticks. He named everything off as he pocketed them. "Wallet, passport, and phone. Check, check, and, ow, check." Bending to slip his wallet into his back pocket hurt.

Now, I can get home...as long as airport security doesn't ask me why I look like hamburger meat.

If they did inquire about his physical state, he would blame it on the passion of a woman he had just met. It was a hundred percent accurate too. Everything that occurred was because of Emma's lust for power. He sighed and laughed at being alive—until his gun was shot out of his hand. The report startled him, as did the clang of the round striking the weapon's steel slide. Jack turned and found Emma standing there, eyes darting back and forth between him and her inert sibling.

Jack's hands went up. "He's fine, well, no, not fine." She raised her gun with unblinking eyes. "He's alive—just out cold."

She pulled the trigger.

He shut his eyes and covered his face, waiting for the projectile to tear through his flesh. Emma was too close to miss.

Strangely, nothing happened.

Slowly, he reopened one eye and peeked between his filthy, bloodstained fingers. He watched Emma struggle with her empty magazine. Jack didn't stick around to gloat. He thanked his lucky stars, and bolted in the other direction, but not before snagging his backpack. Then, he was off to the races.

21

Jack ran for his life. He was done fighting, mostly because he was back down to just a knife, and mostly because he had a gun-toting lunatic hurrying after him. Emma shrieked like a banshee, desperately trying to shoot him in the back. Luckily, her emotions were making her a horrid shot. She had gotten lucky and plinked a pistol out of his hand less than a minute ago. Jack prayed that luck didn't return any time soon.

Run, run, run, as fast as you can, you can't catch me, I'm—

The report of a pistol was followed by a buzz of a bullet passing right by his left ear.

He darted right. "Shit!" Maybe her aim wasn't so terrible after all? Either way, he sprinted for the unexplored railway exit, and put on as much speed as he could muster. His bouncing backpack made it difficult. He didn't have the time to stop and slip in on. So, he ran with it awkwardly hanging over one shoulder.

As he moved, he cracked glow sticks and hurled them forward. In their light, he'd gauge his next course of action. Unfortunately, there was nothing ahead of him except more darkness. There wasn't even anything to hide behind. The tunnel was excavated wider on either side than he had seen thus far. It gave him ample running room— Emma as well.

She made her presence known too. Every few seconds, there'd be a shout of vulgar sounding German. Jack figured she was spewing profanities. Why wouldn't she be at this point?

A bullet impacted the left-hand wall, and instead of immediately zigging right, he stayed on a straightened arrow, counted to three, then moved. If his moves became too predictable, Emma was bound to find her mark.

And she did.

Jack was punched in the middle of his back and thrown to the ground. If it weren't for his Kevlar vest, he'd be dead. It was no different than when he was hit in the ribs with two rounds earlier. He hit the ground and slid to a stop on his belly a few feet later, hands by his side. His face was bathed in the aura of one of his orange glow sticks.

"Ugh," he mumbled, getting a hand up and turning over.

He flopped onto his back and wheezed. Whatever air that had been in his lungs was forcibly expelled. His ungraceful landing didn't help either. The fall opened another cut on the side of his head. If he wasn't a bloodied mess before, he certainly was now.

"Aw, poor Jack."

And now he had to deal with a triumphant sociopath. He wouldn't be fighting back—not this time. If Emma decided that it was his time to die, then let it be done.

By Jack's count, he had killed eleven of her men, give or take one. She had every right to want him dead. If their roles were reversed, he would've felt the same, though, Jack would've never stooped to her low. She was the villain, and he was the hero, plain and simple. Jack was never and would never be the "bad guy."

He would never be like Emma.

"Wipe that smile off your face, witch," he said, pointing a shaky finger at her.

Emma's grin faded. It was replaced by a look that he had seen from her several times already. Rage.

"This is it, Jack," she said, raising her pistol. "Are there any other insults you'd like to hurl my way before I end your miserable life?" She stepped closer. "Anything at all?"

"Actually, yeah," he said, pausing as something slid onto his right foot. He had no idea what it was, and he couldn't see it without moving to check. His first thought was that it was a type of snake, but he couldn't tell what kind. It could've also been something random blowing down the tunnel. There was a slight breeze coming from behind him, deeper into the unknown. Regardless, his Kevlar vest made his body too bulky to dip his chin and glance down to look. So, he asked Emma. Maybe he could keep her talking long enough to think of an escape plan.

"What's on my foot?"

Emma flashed her eyes down toward Jack's feet as, whatever it was, started to move again. The thing wasn't trash. It was alive. He snapped his foot into the air and tossed the creature towards her head. Jack's soccer skills had just paid off. The three-foot-long, brown snake latched onto Emma's throat. The European viper's zigzag pattern was unmistakable. It was also highly venomous and one of the deadliest animals in the region.

Emma reacted as Jack expected. She grabbed at the serpent with both hands, dropping her gun to do so. Seeing it freefall, Jack painfully sat up, and caught the pistol. He repositioned it in his sweaty palms, leveled it up toward her face and pulled the trigger. The bullet exploded from the Glock's barrel and impacted Emma's forehead, entering her skull with little trouble. Brain matter and bone fragments splattered all over the tunnel as the projectile exited through the back of her head.

Gun in hand, Jack flopped to the ground and giggled. There wasn't anything funny about what had just happened. Jack was laughing because he was happy to be alive. He didn't care where the viper had ended up, either. He'd deal with it when, or if, the little shit caused any more trouble. For now, Jack stayed put and rested.

"How'd you get in here?" Jack asked, thinking of the snake.

Probably came down here to get out of the cold.

He sat up and followed the animal as it slithered toward the treasure room. If the creature had gotten in, maybe Jack could get out. Climbing to his feet, he unstrapped his vest. He no longer needed it. The only things he held onto were Emma's pistol, his remaining glow sticks, both of his knives, and his backpack. Next, he somberly reached down and procured Emma's chest-mounted, right-angle flashlight from her vest.

Jack showed it over the entire space, looking for where the serpent had entered. He walked up and down the immediate area and searched for a way out. Sadly, he found nothing and headed north instead. At least, he thought it was north. Still, the viper had to have gotten in from somewhere.

Before Jack started his hike, he started a timer on his watch. His feet ached, but not as much as the rest of him. He plodded along for an hour before finally seeing something promising. There was a rectangularly-cut passage in the right-hand wall of the tunnel. Jack hurried toward it and was filled with glee.

"Stairs..." he said, wishing he was hydrated enough to cry.

He followed them up with his light and saw that a cave-in blocked most of the path. The sight pissed him off more than anything had so far—and that was saying a lot. Midway through his tantrum, he stopped and looked back up the flight. If Jurgen's pack was similar to Karl's, then it would have a key to this lock.

Jack slipped out of his pack and unzipped it, diving into a compartment he had yet to check. He smiled when he found what he needed. Inside the rectangular case were two bricks of plastic explosives. He ascended the steps and jammed one of the clumps as deep as he could. Next came the required blasting cap and timer.

He rushed further up the tunnel and waited, counting down on his wristwatch. In its glow, he read, "Two, one, zero," and covered his ears with his hands. The powerful *whump* was mostly contained by the stone surrounding the staircase. Jack watched as thousands of pounds of rock came crashing down into the tunnel. Some of them even reached the train tracks.

Jack waited for the debris and dust to settle before checking it out. He climbed up and over boulders en route to what he hoped was his escape. The way was still cluttered, but he found an available passage atop the bottleneck. It was so cramped that he was forced to remove his pack and push it along in front of him. Forty feet later, he hit another blockage.

"Come on, man!" he shouted, bashing the base of his fist on the wall to his right.

He dug back into his pack and removed the last of his explosives, setting them with a lengthy timer. He retreated as fast as he could and made it back to the tunnel with plenty of time to spare. Two minutes later, a second, quieter *whump* burst into the hidden world. With very little hope, Jack waddled back over to the stairwell and looked up the substantial incline. He couldn't believe what he saw.

Light.

He practically dove into the obstructed path, dragging his belongings along with him. Up ahead, the path to freedom opened, and it put Jack's mind at ease. Now, he was able to move on his hands and knees, though his footing was uneven and chaotic. It gave twice under his weight. He was getting too ahead of himself. So, he slowed and took more care. The last thing he needed was an inadvertent collapsing.

"Easy does it, Jack." The light grew brighter. "You're almost done."

Or so he hoped.

Even though he had just told himself to take it easy, Jack's pace increased the closer he got to the light. Then, like Gaia herself was birthing him, Jack spilled forward. He landed in a snowy field and slid ten feet before coming to a rest against a tall, leafless tree.

The sky was still light, though the sun was beginning to set. It was peaceful, wherever he was. Curious, Jack sat up and discovered that he was deep inside somebody's backyard. The farm was enormous, settling up against the base of a rise of stone. It seemed that a secondary entrance into the famed Nazi gold train's tunnel had been hidden in plain sight for nearly a century. If Jack had to guess, the owners of this land, at one point, had been Nazi sympathizers, like Piotr. He peered up at his exit but couldn't see anything besides a crumbled hole. Whatever veiled doorway had been there, it was gone now.

He used the tree to get to his feet. Once there, he felt rejuvenated. The cold did wonders for you in some cases. And in others, it was depressing as shit. Now, Jack felt alive—because he was! He had been so close to death several times since meeting Emma.

Jack dug into his pocket, unlocked his iPhone, and opened the Maps app, quickly locating Auschwitz. He smiled when he saw that he was only four miles to the northwest of it. He turned in that direction, toward the Owl Mountains, and wondered what could be there, if anything at all. Now, Jack believed that the Owl Mountains had been a ploy to get people to think that it was where the gold train was located in order to keep treasure hunters off the scent. After all, it was Adolf Hitler who once said, "If you tell a big enough lie and tell it frequently enough, it will be believed."

Jack stepped away from the newly opened fissure just as it collapsed, reburying itself for what he hoped was another eighty years. He vowed to tell no one of what he had found. It was too valuable in too many ways for modern man to have it. For now, Jack would allow his discovery to remain a secret.

Maybe I'll see you again.

He hoped the Auschwitz security team would do the same. Jack had purposely failed to mention the treasure to them, and he had a feeling that Piotr wouldn't be taken seriously. A Nazi sympathizer screaming about a gold train beneath Auschwitz sounded ridiculous—all while being arrested for terroristic activities. The park would hire a new director, one that would have no knowledge of the train's location, or the secret entry within the Cellars. Jack was confident in that. Plus, Jack still had Piotr's key.

The Nazi gold train, as well as the Templar treasure, would remain untouched.

"Woulda been nice to have a slice of it."

He grinned, and his eyebrows lifted, remembering the half dozen handfuls of gold coins he had thrown into his pack. The plan had been to use them as a distraction against Emma while he got away. The opportunity had never come, though. As an alternative, Jack now possessed a memento to his discovery of the grandest collection of antiquities in history. It made him think of what else could be out there. He might just have to look into it.

"You never know." He knelt and scooped up a handful of snow. Gently, he pressed it up against his face, and sighed. "You never know..."

Jack arrived back at Auschwitz an hour later. Along the way, he had continued to treat his injuries with snow. It had stung terribly but it helped numb some of the discomfort. It also brought down a little of the swelling. Luckily, there were large mounds of it on the way to his rental car. Now, all he needed was a fistful of ibuprofen and a stiff drink, and he'd be set.

Climbing inside the SUV, he spotted someone that made him smile. The teenage girl that had helped him up was just now leaving the complex, presumably after being questioned by police. The latter's presence was everywhere. Thankfully, they were more engaged in the camp itself than the people roaming around the parking lot.

She spotted Jack and waved enthusiastically. He returned her wave with a wink and playful salute. The exchange was quick, but it spoke volumes.

Jack practically fell into his rental. Settling in, he called Bull. His partner was the only person he knew he could talk to about what he'd just been through. As Jack pulled out of his parking spot, he glanced down at his bracelets.

Strength and courage.

It made him smile. Jack knew that if shit hit the fan, no matter where he was, that he would always stand for what they represented.

Strength and courage.

EPILOGUE

Two Hours Later

He kicked awake and raised his empty hand. The last thing he remembered was leveling his pistol at Jack. *No,* he thought, tearing away someone else's Kevlar vest from around his head, *that's not right.*

Gunter recalled so much more between then and now, and it enraged him. The American had proven to be a worthy adversary, which shouldn't have surprised him. The man was a former counterterrorism specialist, according to his sister. Not only were Special Forces soldiers exemplary in almost all combat scenarios, but they were smart. Jack displayed both qualities several times.

"Emma!" he shouted. His throat was dry.

No answer.

He slowly climbed to his feet, his head feeling like he was on a turbulent plane ride. The pressure squeezing his skull was nauseating, and his ears were plugged.

A concussion.

Each step he took felt like a jackhammer to the temple. He tried to blink away the discomfort but to no avail. The pain was excruciating. He needed rest and a fifth of vodka.

"Emma?"

He and his sister needed to regroup and go home. The mission had been a disaster. The smart thing to do was fall back and try again at a later date. At least they had confirmed that the treasure existed. Next time, they'd start from the finish and work backward and avoid Auschwitz altogether.

"And next time, I'll kill Jack Reilly myself."

The man was nowhere to be seen. *What would a normal man do in this instance?*

"Go home," Gunter said, stepping lightly.

Maybe I can find where he lives.

His head cleared with every footfall, but the pain didn't. It was something he could deal with. *So could Jack.* Until today, Gunter didn't know humans could have that high of a tolerance to pain.

Gunter headed for the unexplored exit tunnel and stumbled along. He followed a trail of glow sticks until he saw a lump next to the tracks. It wasn't Jack. Somehow, he knew.

"No, no, no..." he muttered, running to the body. Once he saw the blonde hair, Gunter knew it was his sister. "Emma, no."

The sight broke his heart. Emma was his everything, his reason to live. Gunter had kept his anger, and his alcoholism, under control because of his baby sister's focus and her passion. After she had bailed him out of jail three years ago, he decided to rededicate himself to her and her goal. Emma wanted the world.

Tears flowed. With no one around, he openly mourned his fallen sibling. Glancing behind him, Gunter realized that the treasure was all his if he so chose to claim it.

"No," he said, refocusing on cause of his sister's death.

The priceless treasure wasn't Gunter's priority—not anymore. Now, all he cared about was vengeance. He wanted Jack Reilly's head. The thought of killing him brought a smile to Gunter's face. Something slipped into the forefront of his mind. He picked his head up and, once again, looked at the fortune. Then, back to Emma.

His smile grew broader.

Gunter would use some of the wealth behind him, as much as he could carry, and see to it that the American dog died the most excruciatingly painful death imaginable.

Breathing heavily, he stood and snarled. "I'm coming for you, Jack. I'm coming..."

German-occupied Poland
April 30th, 1945

Deputy Commandant of Auschwitz Klaus Wagner's hand trembled. The smell of his smoking Luger was unbearable. It made him sick to his stomach. He had seen enough death for ten lifetimes, though, this was the first time he had ended someone's existence by his own hand. Usually, he would've given an order, and someone else would've taken care of it.

Thirteen lives gone. He had stashed the corpses behind a row of handcarts. Now alone, Klaus had been forced to move them himself.

He knew he could never go back to his family now. Klaus' presence would only jeopardize them more. Sadness gripped his heart. He'd never be able to see little Piotr grow up. Deep down, he hoped his son would stay away from this life. It was a gut-wrenching one.

He stood on the tracks and faced the train station. Behind him, further down the main tunnel, was the treasure room, in all of its glory. His pack sat on the platform, already bursting at the seams with gold. Glancing up the stairs to the bunker, he visualized the messenger he had just killed.

Two hours ago, the young soldier had come rushing through a secondary exit. The closest one sat ahead of the parked train. The access point had been concealed at the rear of a farm. Its owners, the soldier's family, had happily agreed to watch over it.

Panicked, the messenger shouted, "The *Fuhrer* is dead! The *Fuhrer* is dead!"

He had immediately sought out Klaus, the highest-ranking official left, handing him a communique from Berlin. The author was none other than Martin Bormann, Hitler's private secretary, the man who controlled all information to and from the Fuhrer. Some said that Bormann was actually the most powerful man in all of Germany. Information was vital, and Bormann decided what got through.

Breathing hard, eyes wide, Klaus was still trying to unravel what he had done. He holstered his pistol and turned around, shocked by what greeted him. There was a figure standing there, his face veiled by the natural shadows of the dimly lit subterranean world. The insignias on his collar gave away his identity. They were plain to see-as was the pistol gripped in his hand.

"*Reichsfuhrer*," Klaus asked, raising his hands, "is that you?"

Heinrich Himmler stepped out of the shadows and fully revealed himself. He was still wearing his formal uniform, though it was torn in some places and filthy. It was clear that the once-powerful Nazi officer had been on the lam for quite some time. But the hardships he may have faced didn't seem to dull his focus. The man's eyes were as sharp and as intense as ever.

"Yes," Himmler said, smiling like a shark, "but please, there are no pleasantries needed here. I am just Heinrich to you to now."

Klaus swallowed and slowly dropped his hands. In response, Himmler lowered his Luger. "And your standing with the *Fuhrer*?"

Himmler's left cheek twitched. "It is...complicated."

Everyone in the party had heard of Himmler's treachery against Hitler. It didn't matter, though. The Fuhrer was dead, and without a figurehead at the top, everyone was more or less on their own. And Himmler was armed, and he was not a man to trifle with. Ever.

"What will you do?" Klaus asked, curious.

Himmler shrugged. "Hide for as long as I can. I will emerge when things calm down aboveground."

The deputy commandant didn't like the fact that Himmler showed up the day Hitler died. This wasn't just sheer luck. Klaus knew it must've been more than that. His eyes opened wide in realization.

"You knew about this, didn't you?" Himmler didn't react, but nor did he shoot Klaus for suggesting it. "This—all of this—was a plan."

The right corner of Himmler's mouth curled upward. "Yes, *Herr* Wagner, there were contingencies set into motion if the *Fuhrer* or I died before we could move the treasure to our vault beneath the mountains. There were a select few that were made aware of this for obvious reasons."

"Like Martin Bormann?" The man who had ordered Klaus to open fire on his own men. Klaus was livid. "I killed them all—I did!" He jammed a finger in his chest. "None of these men deserved to die today. They were loyal to the *Reich*!"

Himmler's face soured. "Why does any of this surprise you? After everything you've done for the *Fuhrer*, after all the deaths you oversaw here, this is what has shaken your faith?"

"What about you?" Klaus asked, pointing at Himmler. The former Reichsfuhrer gripped his gun harder, but he didn't lift it. Instead, it still hung in his hand down by his side. Klaus tried to hold back his anger but failed. "We have all heard about what you have done."

He waited to be shot, but surprisingly, Himmler held his ground. The man sighed. "We all do what we must to survive. My life was never tied to that man," he stepped forward, "and neither was yours." He smiled. "Stay with me, Klaus."

"What?" Klaus shocked. "No!"

"We will be richer than kings—richer than Hitler ever was."

"No," Klaus repeated. "I have a family. I...I can't leave them behind." He couldn't tell Himmler that it was precisely what he planned on doing. If his falsehood was discovered, he'd be killed for lying. The Reichsfuhrer wasn't always the most understanding man.

"Fine," Himmler replied, bitter, "then be gone with you."

Himmler wasn't happy, but he, nonetheless, stepped aside and watched as Klaus gathered his belongings from atop the platform, then speedily disappeared down the tunnel. The man looked back every few feet to make sure that he didn't get shot in the back.

Himmler wasn't going to kill him, nor could he. His gun was empty.

He smiled slyly. *Klaus didn't know that, though.*

Holstering his spent weapon, Himmler waited for Klaus to distance himself. After a few minutes of inaction, he spun on a heel and hurried toward the collection of valuables he had not seen in some time. Years had passed since he set foot inside her womb. Now, it was all his.

His tour of the bulging treasure room was short but sweet. He imagined what he'd buy while only spending a fraction of what was there. Himmler planned on retiring for the night, but not before finding a change of clothes. His formal uniform was disgusting and something he never planned on wearing again. He planned on burning it as soon as he removed it from his weary body.

After climbing atop the train station platform, Himmler sighed. He wasn't the least bit tired. He looked around and decided to do a little exploring before settling in. The tunnel behind the row of handcarts piqued his interest. He'd only been into the major cavities of the bunker and the treasure room. The rest of the tunnel system was very much alien to him.

Himmler marched off, not paying attention to the pile of fresh corpses to his right. Klaus had done an admirable job, silencing anyone that might want to steal the fortune out from under Hitler's nose.

He grinned. *From 'my' nose.*

Carefully, he jumped down from the platform, and pushed on. He found a fascinating tributary to his right, further into the tunnel.

Hmmm.

Himmler clicked on his large, clunky flashlight, got down on his hands and knees and entered, squeezing into the crevasse. He inched through, reveling in the freedom he was feeling. Himmler was his own man again. This was his life now, and he loved it.

A large, naturally cut chamber greeted him at the end of the trek. He took a moment to collect himself. He felt good.

He stopped, tipped his head up, and breathed. Freedom never smelled so sweet. Never in his adult life did he think he'd be on his own, away from the Nazis, and his beloved SS. Himmler loved his role and his men. However, his love for Hitler's rule had waned over the years.

The one thing that still bothered Himmler more than anything was the Fuhrer's supposed death. Himmler himself was alive because his faithful body double had been captured instead of him. They had made the switch at the last second. The decision had saved Himmler from a crippling fate.

Yesterday, April 29th, Hitler declared that both Himmler and General Hermann Goring, creator of the Nazi secret police, the Gestapo, were traitors to the Reich. After the Fuhrer went into hiding, abandoning his duties, Goring prematurely attempted to take over the party. Hitler had been furious.

And like me, the Fuhrer always had his stand-in close by.

There was a chance that the body the Allies found in Berlin wasn't Adolf Hitler's. Himmler knew, for a fact, that the Fuhrer's dental records and other crucial medical records had been falsified years ago. He knew this because his own files had been covertly changed as well. Himmler forced away the nerve-racking thought and explored more, making it to the center of the room with ease.

If only I had my journal, he thought, regretting sending it to Elias Schmidt. He would've loved to add to it while he was here.

A crack of thunder exploded all around him, and he flopped to the ground. The last thing he saw before his vision faded into nothingness was Klaus Wagner standing over him, smoking pistol in hand.

"Sorry, Heinrich," Klaus said, "but I can't let you have any of this."

Henrich Himmler was dead.

ABOUT THE AUTHOR

MATT JAMES is the international bestselling author of more than twenty action-packed titles (published in multiple languages), including THE FORGOTTEN FORTUNE, CRADLE OF DEATH, DARK ISLAND, SUB-ZERO, THE DRAGON, and the intense DEAD MOON post-apocalyptic series. Matt has also partnered with *USA Today* bestselling author David Wood, co-writing BERSERK, SKIN AND BONES, and LOST CITY.

He dabbles in some graphic design work, creating book covers for authors all over the world. He has designed the vast majority of his own releases.

Matt lives in South Florida with his wife and daughters, enjoying pizza, cold beer, and the work of his favorite authors (Greig Beck, Jeremy Robinson, Ernest Dempsey, Matthew Reilly, and James Rollins).

YOU CAN VISIT MATT AT:

Facebook.com/MattJamesAuthor
Instagram: MattJames_Author
Twitter: MJames_Books

Made in the USA
Columbia, SC
30 July 2023

21032651R00093